An Ames County Novel

A Village Looks Ahead

Reviving a Town, Rekindling a Spirit

JERRY APPS

LITTLE CREEK PRESS
MINERAL POINT, WISCONSIN

Copyright © 2025 Jerry Apps

All rights reserved. No part of this publication may be reproduced, distributed, or transmitted in any form or by any means, including photocopying, recording, digital scanning, or other electronic or mechanical methods, without the prior written permission of the publisher, except in the case of brief quotations embodied in critical reviews and certain other noncommercial uses permitted by copyright law. For permission requests or other information, please send correspondence to the following address:

Little Creek Press
5341 Sunny Ridge Road
Mineral Point, WI 53565

Printed in the United States of America

Cataloging-in-Publication Data
Names: Jerry Apps, author
Title: A Village Looks Ahead
Description: Mineral Point, WI Little Creek Press, 2025
Identifiers: LCCN: 2025946348 | ISBN: 978-1-967311-94-1
Classification: Fiction / Small Town & Rural
FICTION / Family Life / General
FICTION / Literary

Book design by Little Creek Press

For my late wife, Ruth, who helped
me with all of my writing projects,
including this one.

Contents

Prologue . . . .
1: Bank Robbery 3
2: Jackie Jo Jensen 6
3: First Day of Work 11
4: Fred and Oscar 18
5: Writing Class 23
6: Who Has the Money? .29
7: Community Meeting 34
8: Radio WLLK 38
9: Fred and Oscar 41
10: Dexter Comes to Town 46
11: Break Up 53
12: Fred and Oscar 56
13: Writing Class 59
14: Community Meeting 63
15: Radio WLLK 68

16: Fred and Oscar 71

17: Writing Class 73

18: Preacher Increase Joseph 77

19: Flood 81

20: Emergency 84

21: Fred and Oscar 87

22: Radio WLLK 90

23: Ben Neverson 92

24: Chat with the Mayor 97

25: Ben Meets Jackie Jo 101

26: Radio WLLK 105

27: Fred and Oscar 109

28: Ben and Jackie Jo 111

29: Recall Election 115

30: Radio WLLK 118

31: Ben and Jackie Jo 120

32: Radio WLLK 124

33: Fred and Oscar 128

34: Ben and Jackie Jo 131

35: Recall Election 135

36: Election Results 138

37: Fred and Oscar 141

38: Ben and Jackie Jo 143

39: Tornado 147

40: Storm Damage 151

41: Fred and Oscar 153

42: Wedding 156

43: A Village Looking Ahead 160

Epilogue 163

Acknowledgments 166

About the Author 167

Prologue

Change in Midwestern rural communities has come slowly but nonetheless relentlessly as farming and agriculture have profoundly changed, resulting in dramatic adjustments in the countryside as well as in the nearby villages. Seventy-five years ago small family farms dotted the Midwest; now, only a few large farms remain. These earlier farmers were diversified, meaning they raised livestock—beef, sheep, and hogs—perhaps milked some dairy cows, had a small chicken flock, and raised a small acreage of cash crops such as potatoes, cucumbers, green beans, or other canning crops. Today, single-commodity agriculture has become the norm. Most large farms focus on one enterprise—a dairy, poultry, beef, hog, vegetable, or commodity grains operation.

Organic farmers, who do not use pesticides, commercial fertilizers, and other technologies and have relatively small operations, are a major exception. Another exception is so-called hobby farmers, who have full-time jobs off the farm and till small acreages. Another expanding group includes small-acreage vegetable farmers who are responding to the "farm to table" movement, where an increasing number of urban families want their food grown nearby rather than transported from distant places in the country, or even from other countries. Not to be forgotten are the Amish farmers who farm as their ancestors farmed, avoiding the use of nearly all widely accepted technologies, such as electricity and tractors.

As the number of farms declined, the nearby villages (many with populations of one thousand or less) lost business. Farmers depended on these villages for supplies, medical help, a market for their products, and the gristmill to grind feed for their livestock. It was in these villages where farmers bought seeds, fertilizer, lumber, and other necessities to keep their farms operating and their families clothed and healthy. With the decline of small family farms, hardware stores closed, gristmills ceased operating, cheese factory buildings were abandoned, lumberyards slammed shut their doors, and villages struggled to figure out how to survive when their farmer customers disappeared.

In fictional Link Lake, Wisconsin, we meet a group of local citizens who have experienced dramatic changes in their community but have not taken time to examine them or think about the consequences of these changes for their own lives and for the future of their village. As several of them work together in a library-sponsored writing class, they discover things about themselves, their neighbors, and their community that both delight and alarm them.

At the same time that the writing class members are discovering and bringing to light the community's history, a second group, led by Link Lake's mayor, Jon Jessup, is examining Link Lake's current situation and exploring avenues for the community's future. Jessup, a retired (really fired) former city planner, is interested in the community exploring how it can become more self-sufficient in everything from people growing more of their own food to the community exploring ways of generating its own electricity and becoming more environmentally conscious as it moves into the future.

As the two groups—Link Lake Writers and Creating the Future Commission, as the mayor's group is called—learn about each other's efforts, there is a clash of yesterday with tomorrow.

1
Bank Robbery

October 7, 1940

Kaboom! The explosion echoed down Link Lake's Main Street, rattled the windows as far away as Oscar Anderson's farm located a mile from town, and set dogs to barking on this pre-dawn morning in October.

Marshal Lars (Shorty) Haugen, asleep in the little room at the back of the jail, had only been asleep for a few hours when the explosion awakened him. Most nights he didn't get to bed much before two in the morning as he waited for the taverns in Link Lake to close and their customers to make their way home safely. It was potato harvesting season, and the town was filled with extra men brought in to help dig potatoes, so now his nights were even longer.

The marshal jerked awake. "What in hell was that?" he muttered, quickly pulling on his pants and shirt, to which his silver marshal's badge was attached. He slid his suspenders over his shoulders, pulled on his boots, and strapped on the .45 Colt pistol he kept on his nightstand. Then he slipped on his old felt hat and reached for the back door of the jail, his black hair sticking out from under his hat in all directions.

He caught sight of men running down Main Street toward the direction of the explosion, pulling on shirts and jackets as they ran.

"What happened?" the marshal asked the first person he saw.

"Don't know," the man replied. "Somethin' blew up."

"Where's the damn marshal?" came a loud voice from the direction of the Link Lake State Bank. "Where in hell is the marshal when you need him?"

"Over here," Shorty said. He was so out of breath he could scarcely talk. "I'm over here," he repeated as he waved his hand and continued running.

"Well, get your sorry ass over here and right now," the loud voice said from the steps of the bank. The voice was that of Einer Voll, bank president. His round face was red, and his ample middle bulged against the striped nightshirt he wore. His bare feet were stuck in black, untied shoes.

"What can I do for you?" The marshal said, hardly able to speak the words as he was so out of breath. A thread of gray smoke trickled out of the open bank door, and the marshal could see that the bank's front windows were broken.

"The bank's been robbed," Voll yelled so loudly that the marshal stumbled back a couple steps.

"Bank robbed?" the marshal stammered.

"Yeah, you dumb ass. The bank's been cleaned out. Every last nickel scraped up and taken. Safe all blown to hell."

All the marshal could think to say was, "Is that so?"

"Well, what are you gonna do about it?" the banker yelled.

"I … I … I don't know," stammered the marshal. At that moment the marshal wished he had slipped some bullets in his pocket. Ordinarily, he carried his revolver unloaded—safer for all concerned. He sometimes remembered to stick half a dozen bullets in his pocket, but lately he'd had no call to shoot at anything, so he usually forgot the bullets. Last time he shot his pistol was when Mable Anderson's dog cornered a skunk behind her woodpile, and she ran over to the marshal's office for help. He shot the skunk twice and wished he hadn't. Stunk up the whole neighborhood for most of a month.

"Well, Marshal. We haven' got all day. You want us to form up a posse or what?" the banker said loudly.

The marshal racked his brain, trying to remember what he had learned about bank robberies from the National Peace Officers Correspondence School that he had enrolled in last January when he was first appointed marshal. He was quite sure he hadn't got that far in the course.

"Yeah, let's get ourselves a posse," the marshal blurted out. "Gotta find them bastards that done this." The marshal drew himself up to his full five feet four inches and fingered the handle of his pistol. He was trying to think of an excuse to slip back to the jail and pick up some bullets.

2
Jackie Jo Jensen

A year ago, on January 2, Jackie Jo Jensen started work as head librarian at the Increase Joseph Memorial Library in Link Lake, Wisconsin. It was her first job after graduating from the University of Wisconsin–Madison with a degree in library science and a minor in English. She felt exceedingly lucky because jobs were scarce, especially in library science, and she looked forward to receiving a paycheck after all those years of schooling.

Jackie Jo grew up in Columbus, Ohio, where her parents were professors at The Ohio State University. She was an only child, and while in high school, she had decided that she needed to get away from Columbus and the shadow of The Ohio State University, which had been the family's life for as long as she could remember. She had always been interested in books and, while in high school, had worked at her local library as a page. Her friends often kidded her if she would be able to work her way up to being a "Table of Contents," but she considered that the lamest of jokes.

When she told her high school counselor that she was interested in becoming a librarian or a novelist, her counselor suggested she enroll at the University of Wisconsin–Madison in their library science program and then minor in English. There she could pursue both interests.

While at UW–Madison, Jackie Jo met Dexter Wilson, an English major. Dexter was from Chicago. He had graduated the same day as Jackie Jo and began driving a cab and working on the great American novel. When Jackie Jo told Dexter she'd gotten this job as a librarian in Link Lake, Wisconsin, beating out thirty-five other applicants, he laughed.

"Where in the world is Link Lake, and why would anyone want to work there?"

She told him it was only one hundred miles north of Madison and not all that difficult to find, and it was a job. "In my major, besides," she pointed out to him. He let that last comment float right over his head.

When he asked Jackie Jo how big Link Lake was and she told him it was 1,500 people, he laughed louder than ever. She couldn't blame him too much because, having grown up in Columbus, Ohio, she remembered more than once hearing about how rural America was dragging down the rest of the country with its old ways of thinking and doing and how rural people were reluctant to do anything that looked at all like progress. She also remembered once saying to Dexter that rural folks were so caught up with their old-time religion, outdated values, and misinformed beliefs that they would forever remain mired in their histories.

But she also remembered the nice people who interviewed her for the library job. There had been just two: Jon Jessup, mayor of Link Lake, and Carolyn Stevens, president of the library board. They offered to meet Jackie Jo at a restaurant in Montello, as the mayor said, "So you don't have to drive all the way through the cold and snow to Link Lake."

She remembered the interview well. The mayor had asked her if she had ever lived in a rural community, and she had answered that she hadn't but was looking forward to it. Carolyn, a forty-something mother of three school-age kids, said with a pleasant smile, "We're so pleased that you are interested in becoming our new librarian. Do you like books?"

Jackie Jo thought the question was a little silly. "Of course," she said. "Always have." She wondered if there was more to the question, such as, "What's your take on banned books?" "What about books that have homosexual characters?" "What about books filled with sex and violence?" "What about books that present information about religions that are not Christianity?" But Carolyn didn't follow up with further questions. Mostly they talked about the Village of Link Lake, what a great little place it was, and how people liked and have always supported the library.

The day after the interview, the mayor called Jackie Jo and said she was the new librarian at the Increase Joseph Memorial Library and that she should plan to start work on January 2.

"So why in heaven's name did you take the job?" Dexter had asked.

"Well, Dex," she told him, "truth be known, I don't expect to be very busy, so I will have time to work on my novel." She emphasized the word *my* because she and Dex had always been a bit competitive when it came to writing. Besides, she figured she'd have more time to write than he did driving a cab. Then she told him that she thought she could take working in little backwater Link Lake for a couple of years before she found a better job, and in the meantime, she should have time to work on her novel.

Jackie Jo remembers all these things as she walked from her little apartment toward the Increase Joseph Memorial Library and her first day of work a year ago. She had driven to Link Lake the previous evening. Her first time in the village. It was an easy drive from Madison. She motored along Highway 22 for a couple of hours, slowed down for several small towns, drove through Montello, and before she could think about a main character for the novel, she was in Link Lake. She discovered that the highway crowded the south shore of the big lake after which the village was named. She spotted a few lights blinking from the opposite shore—tiny beacons on a dark night. She drove past the Quick Stop Convenience Store, past the Link Lake Post Office—a little one-story nondescript building with a blue mailbox out front. She slowly drove past the Link Lake Tap, with four cars parked near its door, and past the Black Oak Café, with three cars there. A bit farther on, she passed the Link Lake Hotel, which anchors the south end of Main Street—a sturdy old building with a red neon light that shouted "vacancy" into the dark night. She noticed the other buildings on Main Street were dark, including a big two-story brick building with a lighted sign that read "Antiques" and a faded white sign above it that said "Link Lake Mercantile."

She easily found the Williams House following the directions that Mayor Jessup had given her. At the Williams House, she had rented a two-room apartment sight unseen but highly recommended by the mayor. Emily and Ethyl Williams, twins who never married, owned and operated Williams House. Emily had taken her up to the little two-room apartment on the second floor of which she said was in "one of the oldest houses in Link Lake." Emily was tall and thin, with gray hair fastened in a bun on top of her head. Emily said that Jackie Jo would meet Ethyl the following morning, as she was a paid volunteer at the library, whatever that meant.

Jackie Jo remembers walking two blocks down Main Street and another block on Link Avenue. Just as she was today, a year later. She had arrived at the library at eight-thirty, an hour early, as the library opened at nine-thirty. She noticed the lights were on and the door unlocked.

"Good morning, Miss Jensen."

She was taken a bit by surprise, as she didn't expect to meet anyone. She was also a bit surprised because the person who greeted her looked exactly like her landlady.

"I'm Ethyl Williams. You met Emily last night. We're identical twins, which confuses lots of people." Ethyl even sounded like her sister. She, like her sister, wore her gray hair in a bun.

Jackie Jo extended her hand. "Nice to meet you. I'm looking forward to working with you. And please, call me Jackie Jo."

"If there is anything you want to know about this place, I probably know it. I've been volunteering here for forty years, nearly full-time for the last ten years. Do get paid a little, which is much appreciated. My mother, Phoebe Williams, long deceased, volunteered here before me."

"Thank you so much," Jackie Jo said. "I'll need all the help I can get. By the way, what happened to the previous librarian?"

"Sort of sad it was. Flo—her name was Florence, but we all called her Flo—died right here in the library. She was our librarian for forty years, and we'd just had a little celebration for her. Place was filled with library patrons all shaking her hand and hugging her, and telling her what a great job she was doing and how everyone was looking forward to working with her for years to come."

"What happened?" Jackie Jo asked.

"Well, I thought she looked a little pale, and she wasn't acting like her old self, but I considered that the emotion of the party had affected her a little, so I didn't think much of it. Then I saw her walk over by the religious book section carrying a piece of marble cake, the kind that's brown and white. Without so much as a peep, she just keeled over right next to where the Bibles were shelved. Spilled her marble cake on the floor and died right there. Heart attack, the coroner said."

"That's a sad story."

"Guess it is. But we all have to leave sometime, kind of interesting that she'd leave us right there in the religious section. Kind of appropriate, I guess."

3
First Day of Work

Ethyl gave Jackie Jo the grand tour of the place. She showed her the children's reading section, where the young adult books were shelved, the fiction and nonfiction shelves, the large-print section, the rack of DVDs, the reference section, and the computer corner with six computers. She showed her the community room. "Holds up to seventy-five people," Ethyl said proudly. "And here is our kitchen where a noon meal is prepared for the community senior citizens on Mondays, Wednesdays, and Fridays. But I never eat here." She smiled. "I'm waiting until I get old. I'm only seventy-five." Ethyl chuckled.

They walked to the far end of the building, and Ethyl pointed to a closed door. "That's your office and the storage room," she said. "I'll go fetch the books from the book drop. You've got a few minutes before we open the doors. Supposed to open at nine-thirty, but Flo and I always open by nine-fifteen, especially on these cold winter days."

Jackie Jo looked around the little office. Papers, books, and newspapers were piled everywhere so that she couldn't even see the top of the little desk pushed against the wall in front of a window. She looked for a computer but saw none. She surmised that Flo must have used the computer at the circulation desk, or maybe she didn't use one at all. She knew some older people like that. They kept doing things the way they always did them. Maybe Flo was one of those.

Jackie Jo pulled open the desk drawers and found the usual. Paper clips, a yellow notepad, a stapler. She began making piles that she stacked on the floor. A pile of newspapers. A pile of magazines. A pile of paperback books. She wondered why the books weren't in the library. She looked more closely at the cover of one of the books and saw a scantily clad young woman embracing an equally scantily clad young man. She opened the book and read the first line on a page: "His hot breath on my bare skin sent ripples of arousal through every fiber of my body."

She then realized that Flo likely decided what should and should not go on the shelves at the Increase Joseph Memorial Library. There would be no angry parent letters about "dirty books" and instructions to pull them from the shelves if they never made it to the shelves in the first place. She reminded herself that she should ask Ethyl about the paperbacks.

Before Jackie Jo could finish sorting and stacking, it was nine-fifteen, and she heard Ethyl unlocking the door and library patrons entering. She hurried to the circulation counter so the Link Lake community could see that their new librarian was on the job. First through the door was Mayor Jon Jessup.

"Good morning, Mayor Jessup," Jackie Jo said, smiling broadly.

"Call me Jon," he said. "Are you finding everything? Anything you need? We want you to be comfortable."

"Well," she began, wondering if she should mention the lack of a computer in her office on her first day at work. "I noticed that my office does not have a computer," she said quietly so others wouldn't hear.

"I'm not surprised. Flo never used a computer much, only for organizing the collection and checking out books. Said they were too hard to learn. Always did strange things."

"I suppose I can understand that," Jackie Jo said, not really believing that a librarian nowadays didn't spend considerable time on a computer.

"Tell you what," Jessup said. "What if I move one of these computers from the computer section into your office? How would that be?"

Before Jackie Jo could answer, the mayor unplugged the nearest computer, grabbed hold of it, and began carrying it toward her office. "Tell me where you want it," he said over his shoulder as she hurried along behind him.

Jackie Jo opened the office door for him and pointed to a little table near the desk that she had cleared of old newspapers.

"Anything else you can think of right now?" the mayor asked.

"I . . . I don't think so," Jackie Jo said haltingly, surprised at how quickly the mayor had acted.

The mayor and Jackie Jo returned to the circulation desk, where she heard the mayor ask Ethyl if the library had any books on wind farms. She and the mayor went off to check the catalog on the computer while Jackie Jo met the next library patron standing in line.

"My name is Lucy Miller," the well-dressed woman in her seventies, with a high-pitched voice, said.

"I'm Jackie Jo Jensen, your new librarian."

"I'm so pleased to meet you. My late husband was president of the Link Lake Bank and was always a supporter of the library, as am I," she said as she tossed a purple scarf over her shoulder. "Oh, by the way, if I might ask, what church do you attend?"

"What . . . what church?" Jackie Jo answered, wondering why she was asking.

"Oh, I didn't mean to pry—just wanted to be helpful. Help you find your way around the community, get settled in," she babbled on.

"I was raised a Lutheran," Jackie Jo said quietly.

"Oh, that's unfortunate," said Mrs. Miller. "The nearest Lutheran church is in Willow River, and that's eight miles away. Most of us in Link Lake belong to the Church of Peace. Nice church. Great pastor. Good people."

"Well, thank you for letting me know," Jackie Jo said, trying to sound respectful.

"We'll see you on Saturday afternoon," Mrs. Miller said as she turned and left.

Before Jackie Jo had time to think about what she meant by the

Saturday afternoon comment, an older gentleman wearing bib overalls and a red cap came to the counter.

"Name is Fred. Fred Russo. I have a little farm just out of town a bit." He thrust out his hand to shake Jackie Jo's. She noticed the size of his hands and how wrinkled and calloused they were. His handshake was firm but gentle, and as he spoke, he looked Jackie Jo right in the eye. His gray eyes sparkled when he talked. Jackie Jo liked that in people.

"I've been a regular customer of this library for more than seventy years," Fred said. "And I'm so pleased that you are our new librarian. Pretty important job, that of a librarian. Pretty darn important."

Jackie Jo quickly decided that Fred Russo was her kind of guy, even if he was older than her grandfather. Fred walked off toward the newspaper section. As he walked away, he said, "Looking forward to Saturday afternoon."

Now Jackie Jo was becoming even more curious. What was happening on Saturday afternoon?

Next in line was a tall, gray-haired man. "Name is January, spelled just like the month," he said as he reached out to shake her hand. "Joe January, but everybody calls me Bud."

"Well, Bud January, good to meet you."

"I'm a former game warden, worked for the Department of Natural Resources for many years. Love this library."

"I'm Jackie Jo Jensen."

"Yup, I know that. Saw your picture and story in the *Ames County Argus*. If you don't mind my saying, you are even prettier in person than your picture."

Jackie Jo could feel herself blushing a little. "Well, thank you," she said. She didn't realize her photo had been in the local paper.

"I am surely looking forward to Saturday—even more now that I've had a chance to say hello. Oh, remember this. Every day is a good day, except some are better than others."

She must ask Ethyl what was happening on Saturday, but before she could, Ethyl said,

"It's almost ten-thirty. You'd best get ready for the Children's

Morning Story Time." She no more than said it when mothers toting cute little kids began streaming through the door, removing their warm coats and finding a place in the children's reading section. The mothers helped themselves to the coffee that Ethyl had earlier started and then took chairs behind their children, who all sat in a circle on the floor.

Jackie Jo grabbed the first children's picture book she saw on the shelf and sat down on a chair facing eight eager children—five little girls and three little boys.

"My name is Miss Jackie Jo," she said as confidently as she could. "I'm your new librarian."

A little girl wearing a pink sweater and matching pink slacks held up her hand.

"Yes," Jackie Jo said.

"Miss Flo always sat in that rocking chair when she read to us."

"Oh, sorry," Jackie Jo got up, pushed the chair aside, put the rocking chair in place, and opened the book she had picked up. She hadn't even looked at the title. Another hand shot up.

"Do you live here?"

"I do now, but I lived in Madison before moving here. Perhaps we should get started reading."

Jackie Jo began reading *Lilly's Purple Plastic Purse* while holding the book so the children could see the colorful pictures of Lilly and her purse. She read through the book as the children watched and listened; they seemed enthralled by the story. She was obviously doing something right, and she was pleased. She asked if anyone had any questions, and a little hand shot up.

"Yes." She was prepared to answer a question about the book.

"Miss Flo always had graham crackers and chocolate milk for us when she finished reading."

"Oh, I'm sorry. Next week I'll have graham crackers and milk for you." The same little hand went up again.

"It has to be chocolate milk. Some of us don't like regular milk."

"Yes, chocolate milk it is."

The children got up from the floor and began exploring the new

A VILLAGE LOOKS AHEAD

book section in the children's reading area. As they did, one of the mothers came up to Jackie Jo.

"I'm Abigail Johnson, and that was my little boy who was concerned about the graham crackers and chocolate milk. I'm sorry if he embarrassed you."

"No, no problem. Next week there will be graham crackers and chocolate milk." As she said it, she wondered who paid for the weekly treats for the preschoolers.

"Oh, the book you read. That was a good choice. The children always like to hear about Lilly and the purple plastic purse. In fact, that was the last book Miss Flo read to the children—it was the week she died. She was a wonderful librarian. We all miss her so much."

Finally, at noon, when there was a little break between patrons, Jackie Jo approached Ethyl. "What is happening two Saturdays from now? Several people said they'd see me then."

"Oh, for heaven's sake. Didn't anyone tell you? You're teaching a three-hour writing class here at the library. Florence had it all organized before she died. Got several people signed up. You've already met some of them."

"A writing class?" Jackie Jo blurted out.

"The mayor should have told you. I heard it was one of the reasons you were hired—that you have a degree in English."

Jackie Jo watched while Ethyl dug around behind the checkout counter. She found a copy of the *Ames County Argus* and handed it to her. On the front page she saw her picture and the following story:

> **"Link Lake Hires New Librarian"**
>
> *Following the untimely death of beloved librarian Florence Goodnight, Miss Jackie Jo Jensen, formerly of Columbus, Ohio, has been hired as head librarian for the Increase Joseph Memorial Library in Link Lake. Miss Jensen recently completed a degree in library science and English from the University of Wisconsin–Madison and will begin her duties on January 2.*
>
> *For those who may have wondered about the local history writing class that Miss Goodnight organized prior to her demise, it will go on as planned, with the first session scheduled for*

Saturday, January 6 at 1:00 p.m. with the able assistance of Miss Jensen as instructor.

On that same page in the paper, Jackie Jo glanced at another article, which caught her attention.

"Link Lake Mayor Organizes Planning Commission"

Jon Jessup, mayor of Link Lake, has organized a Planning Commission to examine, as Mayor Jessup says, "Where Link Lake, Wisconsin, wants to be in five years." He has asked the following local citizens to be a part of the commission: Gwendolyn James, a former rural sociology professor; Tony Noble, a graduate student in Environmental Education at the University of Wisconsin–Oshkosh, whose parents live in Link Lake; Oscar Anderson, a retired farmer; and Robert Spranger, owner of Spranger Hardware in Link Lake.

The Planning Commission plans to coordinate its activities with the local history writing group being organized at the library.

As Mayor Jessup said, "We can't know where we're going until we know where we've been." But the mayor also cautioned that some towns become stuck in their histories and fail to be forward-looking. "We want to do both in Link Lake. We want to be aware of and learn from our histories, but we also want to boldly look toward the future. Indeed, we want to create our own future."

The commission plans to meet weekly for several weeks and then will begin sharing their results with the larger community.

Jackie Jo put down the newspaper and tried not to let Ethyl see how furious she was about not being told about her teaching assignment. She thought, *I've never taught anything in my life—any kind of class, for kids, for adults, for anyone. I'm not a teacher. I'm a librarian and, I hope, a writer.*

4

Fred and Oscar

Fred Russo and Oscar Anderson meet every Monday morning for coffee at the Black Oak Café on Main Street in Link Lake. The retired farmers are both in their eighties and grew up on neighboring farms and spent their lives working the land.

Tall and slim, Fred wears bib overalls no matter where he goes or what he does. Oscar, shorter and stockier than his friend, never wears bib overalls to town but pulls on the trousers he used to wear to church—he hasn't attended church since his wife died. Oscar, with a full head of gray hair and shorter than Fred, walks with a cane left over from a farm accident that had him laid up for nearly six months.

Both men lost their wives ten years ago to influenza that swept the Link Lake community at the time, but Oscar and Fred remain friends and neighbors. Although they continue to disagree on many things, now in their twilight years, the two old farmers fish together, occasionally hunt together, and every Monday morning, without fail, drink coffee together and talk about anything and everything.

The Black Oak Café is one of the few survivors of the dramatic changes that overtook the Village of Link Lake starting in the 1960s and continuing to the present as farm numbers dwindled and the village struggled to survive. One reason the café continues to do well is because of the urban visitors who stop there for lunch or dinner on their way farther north to vacation. Some visitors think they are in northern Wisconsin when they arrive in Link Lake and camp at the area campgrounds or stay at one of the resorts on Link Lake for a week or two during the summer months.

Pauline Evans, a longtime waitress at the Black Oak, greeted Fred Russo when he arrived.

"Your table is ready," she said. Pauline, who wore her sixty years well, enjoyed Fred and Oscar. Every Monday morning before they arrived, Pauline put a reserved sign in the shape of a little straw hat on their favorite table.

"Looks like old Oscar ain't here yet," muttered Fred as he removed his red Farmall tractor cap and ran his hand through his thick gray hair before hanging his jacket on the back of his chair.

"Nope. Haven't seen him yet," said Pauline. "Can I bring you a cup of coffee?"

"Might's well. Oscar probably slept in this morning. Wouldn't surprise me. He's one of the least dependable old coots I ever knowed."

Pauline smiled as she followed Fred to the reserved table with a coffee pot in one hand and two cups in the other.

"Should I pour Oscar's?"

"Sure. Serve him well to drink cold coffee. Teach him for bein' late for our important Monday meetings." Fred smiled when he said it, for he knew that not much of importance ever transpired at their Monday morning coffee gatherings.

Fred no more than took his first sip of coffee when Oscar showed up at the table, out of breath with his green John Deere cap in one hand and his ever-present cane in the other.

"You're late," Fred said gruffly.

"Got a late start from home," said Oscar. "Had something important I was workin' on."

"You was doin' somethin' important? Can't imagine what that might be. Neither of us has done much that's important for more years than I can count."

"Speak for yourself, Fred. I've been busier than a tomcat on a full-moon night, and it's pretty darn important, too, if I must say so myself."

Oscar hung his cap on the side of the table and hung his jacket over the back of his chair, then sat down, picked up his coffee, and took a big sip.

"So you gonna tell me what's so important that you show up late for our regular Monday morning confab?"

"Wasn't that late. Maybe only five minutes."

"Late is late. No matter if it's five minutes or fifteen minutes, you're still late," said Fred as he picked up his coffee cup.

"You wanna know what I was doin' or not? Or you wanna argue some more about what's late and what's not?" asked Oscar.

"Okay, what've you been up to that's so ding dang important?"

"I'm doin' my homework for the commission the mayor asked me to serve on."

"You what?"

"Crank up your hearing aid, Fred. The mayor asked me to be a part of a commission. He's callin' it the Link Lake Planning Commission," said Oscar.

"Well that's sure a highfalutin name. But what in hell does it mean? If I could be so bold to ask? Tell me, what is a commission anyway?"

"We're a small group that will be lookin' at where the Village of Link Lake is now and where the community wants to be in five years. Sounds pretty interesting, but we haven't met yet. We'll have our first meeting next week."

"Sounds kind of dumb to me. We all know where we're at, and where we're gonna be in five years is where we're gonna be. It's as simple as that."

"Mayor doesn't think so. He believes we can create our own future," said Oscar.

"Sounds like one of those progressive ideas the mayor talked about during his election campaign." Fred said the word *progressive* in the same way he might mention a manure pile out back of his barn.

"Which reminds me," said Oscar, "you remember that I signed you up for the writing class that starts on Saturday at the library. Hope you haven't let the class slip out of that fragile memory of yours, Fred."

Oscar held up his cup for Pauline to see that he needed a warm-up.

"I'm still a little miffed that you signed me up for that dang class. I ain't no writer, never was, never will be. When I see something that looks like a poem, my eyes blur, and my mind goes goofy."

"Fred, this is no class about writing poetry. You're gonna write local history, something about what's gone on here in the greater Link Lake community since it got started back in 1852."

"How'd you know it got started in 1852?"

"One of those things I just know. Studied the history of Link Lake back when I was in high school."

"So you still can remember stuff from high school?"

"Yup. Can't you?"

"Don't think much about high school these days. That was a long time ago. Lots of years passed under the bridge since then," said Fred.

With their coffee cups refilled, both old farmers were quiet for a bit.

"Met the new librarian on Tuesday," said Oscar, breaking the silence. "She's gonna teach the writing course."

"Yeah, I saw the article in the *Argus*," Fred asked. "She a good teacher?"

"Don't know about her teaching abilities, but that Jackie Jo Jensen is a looker."

"Geez, Oscar, one minute you're all excited about me in this dang writing class, and the next thing I hear is that you're ogling the librarian. What's with you? You losing it in your old age?"

"Fred, I may be old, but I ain't blind. I know a well-built woman when I see one."

"Good lord, Oscar. I think you're comin' down with the old-timers disease or whatever it is they call that thing that takes away your senses and messes up your memories."

"Fred, it's Alzheimer's disease, and I don't have it."

"So, Oscar, why did you sign me up for that dang writer's class?"

"Because we need to help folks know how farming has changed these past seventy-five years, that's why. And I know you've got lots of good stories."

"Doesn't everybody know how farmin's changed? Pretty simple. The big farmers got bigger. The rest left, except for a few of us old guys who still live on the land but don't do much farmin'."

"Fred, that's exactly why you need to write down some of what happened—what we remember about how farming changed since we were kids growing up without electricity and milking cows by hand. People need to know about that stuff."

"Don't remember a lot of it," said Fred. "Went by so fast. Kind of a blur, all those changes. Kind of all tangled up together."

"Fred, that's why you're taking the class, to recall your memories and sort them out, and write them down."

"Seems a bit more than I can handle. But I'm looking forward to meeting this new librarian. You might have overlooked the fact that I'm not as blind as you think. Jackie Jo Jensen just might be the ticket to brighten up a cold winter day."

"Now, you're talkin', Fred."

5
Writing Class

Every spare moment Jackie Jo had during her first week on the job as librarian, she had her nose in one of the writing life story books on the library shelves. She read *Telling Your Story, Writing the Memoir,* and *Writing from Your Life.* And she skimmed through many more. Now she had wished that she'd taken a course in creative writing as a part of her English minor, rather than spending all her time analyzing and dissecting nineteenth-century poets and novelists.

She took a couple of the books home every evening, hoping to gain ideas on what she might share on Saturday. She had a sign-up slip for the writing class on the checkout counter, and when she glanced at it Friday evening before leaving for home, she spotted six names. She was glad it wasn't sixteen.

Saturday morning dawned clear and cold, minus ten degrees. Jackie Jo wondered if the cold would keep people away. Maybe even those who signed up might postpone the workshop to a later date. Jackie Jo was at the library promptly at nine o'clock, prepared to take phone calls from people canceling. But there were no calls from people saying they weren't coming and that the workshop should be postponed. Not a single call.

At noon, she began arranging the tables and chairs in the meeting room, now quite sure that every one of the six people who signed up for the writing course was planning to attend. At twelve-thirty they began arriving. First to come through the door was Ezra Brown, a tall, thin, fifty-something man wearing a black shirt and black trousers. He was carrying a small black briefcase.

"I'm Pastor Ezra Brown," he said, smiling.

"Nice meeting you, Miss Jensen. In case you've not heard, I'm pastor of the Church of Peace here in Link Lake."

"Yes, I've heard about your church. It's quite highly regarded."

"Thank you. By the way, have you found Jesus?"

The question stopped Jackie Jo in her tracks. Never before had anyone asked her that question. She wanted to answer, *I didn't know he was lost*, but quickly thought better of it.

"I . . . I haven't thought about it," Jackie Jo stammered.

"Well, you should because your salvation depends on it," said the pastor, still smiling.

"Thank you," was all Jackie Jo could think to say. But she wondered what kind of contribution this guy would make to the writing group.

Thankfully, Carolyn Stevens arrived, and she didn't have to try an answer any more of the pastor's questions.

"Hello, Carolyn," Jackie Jo said. "So glad to see you again." She didn't let on how glad she was to see Carolyn at that moment, to see anyone, as she didn't know what the pastor would ask next.

By a quarter to one, the six members of the writing group had arrived and found their places around the table. She had provided name tags for each person, although she wondered why she needed them as she was quite certain that everyone knew each other.

Jackie Jo began promptly at one o'clock, trying to sound confident and not reveal how dry her mouth was. She could feel the knot in her stomach.

"Welcome," she said. "I'm Jackie Jo Jensen, your new librarian. I've met some of you, but not all, and I'm pleased that you're a part of this group. Some of you are probably wondering about my background. Well, I grew up in Columbus, Ohio. My parents were professors there. To get away from home, I decided to attend the University of Wisconsin in Madison." She smiled when she said it. "And I've just graduated from the UW with a degree in library science with a minor in English. I'm pleased to be here in Link Lake and want to learn more about this village and the people who live here. But enough about me. Mayor Jessup has told me how important your work will be and how the stories you write will be a part of a larger effort he has planned. The mayor said he'd stop by around quarter past one to say a few words."

With the mention of the mayor's appearance, the group wondered how a story they might write would have anything to do with what the mayor had in mind.

"While we're waiting for the mayor, let's take a few minutes to introduce yourselves and say a word about your background. I know most of you probably know each other, but let's do it anyway. Let's start with you, Carolyn."

"I'm Carolyn Stevens, president of the library board. I'm pleased to be part of this group and looking forward to our stories."

"I'm Fred Russo, retired from farming, and have a bunch of farm stories, but I'm no writer. Neighbor signed me up. He said my stories need to be told. So here I am."

"Thank you, Fred," said Jackie, nodding to the next person at the table.

"Joe January," said a tall, thin man with thick gray hair. "Everyone calls me Bud. I was a game warden for the DNR for thirty years. Been retired now for five years. Have a few stories to tell."

"I'm Pastor Ezra Brown, pastor of the Church of Peace here in Link Lake. Pleased to be a part of this group. I believe most of you know Lucy Miller, widow of our longtime bank president, Adolf Miller. Mrs. Miller suggested I join this group. She said to have a well-rounded set of stories about Link Lake, we must know its spiritual history. I couldn't agree more. I am pleased to be here."

"I'm Lucy Miller," said a tiny woman, not even five feet tall, but with a voice that belonged to someone much larger. "My husband, now deceased, was manager of the Ames County Bank here in Link Lake for many years."

"I guess I'm last," said Emily Higgins, an eighty-something woman with a strong, firm voice. "I'm president of the Link Lake Historical Society and more than pleased to be a part of this group."

Right on time, Mayor Jessup poked his head through the door.

"Am I interrupting?" he asked. The mayor had a little box under his arm, which he set down on the table.

"No, no. I told the group you would be coming." Jackie Jo wondered what he had in the box.

"Well, first let me say that I'm more than pleased to see all of you here. You may have read in the *Ames County Argus* about my plans," Jon began. He stood at the end of the table next to Jackie Jo.

"I have in mind a way for the Link Lake community to both look at where it has been as well as look to where it wants to be in five years. As you probably know, we have another group discussing the community's future. As I was quoted in the newspaper, a community cannot know where it's headed until it knows where it's been—to know its history. That's where you folks come in."

The mayor had everyone's attention.

"I've heard many stories about Link Lake's past, but almost none are written down. I see you folks as key to writing down the stories of this community. Your own stories and the stories of your friends and neighbors. I'm so pleased that we've been able to hire a librarian who not only knows how to operate a library but also knows how to help you write your stories and to go out and interview others in the community, especially the old-timers who have the community's history in their heads."

The mayor opened the box and took out several small digital recorders. "I've purchased these little recorders that you can use to record the interviews. Each comes with a sheet of instructions, so you'll have no trouble using them. I have one for you, too, Jackie Jo."

The mayor looked around the room for a reaction. He did not look at Jackie, who sat next to him. If he had, he would have seen a near look of horror. She had worked all week to figure out how to teach basic story-writing skills, and now she was also expected to help this group learn how to interview their friends and neighbors. And to record the interviews with a digital recorder. She had not a clue how to do that. She had never, ever interviewed anyone about anything. She had seen these little digital recorders but had never used one.

"I'll leave you to get on with your workshop. Again, thank you all for agreeing to do this. I look forward to reading your stories and those you gather from others."

The mayor quickly left the room. There was dead silence as the six workshop participants looked at each other and now realized that they were expected to do more than merely jot down a few of their memories.

"Okay, let's get started," Jackie Jo said confidently. "One of the first things in writing down your story is deciding which story to write. For practice, I have an idea. Take a minute to think about your favorite toy when you were a kid."

"I haven't been a kid for a good long time," said Fred Russo, smiling broadly.

"None of us has," chimed in Bud January.

Jackie Jo said nothing for a few moments. "Do you have a favorite toy in mind?"

Pastor Brown raised his hand.

"Yes, Pastor," said Jackie Jo.

"I don't know if this counts as a toy," the pastor began, "but it was the first gift I remember receiving from my mother, and I still have it. I have it with me right now. I always have it with me."

The pastor reached into his briefcase and withdrew a tattered, leather-covered Holy

Bible. "This has been my constant companion since I was a young boy and didn't yet know how to read. It's much more than a toy, of course; it's my guide, my friend, my constant companion on this rugged path we all walk."

"Thank you for sharing," Jackie Jo said. She couldn't think of what else to say and wondered a bit about the kind of contributions the pastor would make to the group.

Bud January raised his hand. "I remember getting a little toy dart gun, the kind where the dart has a suction cup on the end and would stick on a metal target. I was maybe four years old."

A VILLAGE LOOKS AHEAD

"I had a curly-headed doll," said Carolyn Stevens. "I named her Amie, and I carried her with me everywhere. I slept with her. She sat beside me at the table when I ate. I talked to Amie. Sang to her. Even after one of her arms fell off, I didn't mind. Amie was still my constant companion."

A few people chuckled, and most smiled.

"Okay, what I want you to do now is write a story connected with this toy. You have fifteen minutes," instructed Jackie Jo.

When the fifteen minutes were up, she explained to the group that they were doing forced writing, or timed writing. And when they wrote against the clock, they were more likely to energize their creative side, not allowing their judging side to have an opportunity to make comments in their head about how they could or should improve upon what they were doing.

"Did that work for you?" Jackie Jo asked.

Several heads nodded yes.

"Didn't work for me. Something in my head kept saying, *Make sure you spell the words right and put the commas in the right place*," said Fred.

"Try it when you get home, Fred. Set a timer for fifteen minutes, think of a story you want to write, and then keep writing until the bell rings. You might surprise yourself."

"We'll see," said Fred, unsure that Jackie's advice would help him scratch some words down on paper.

"We're almost out of time," continued Jackie Jo. "For our next session, I want you to write a story from your growing-up years. Focus on when you were twelve years old. Bring the story with you to class. And a second part of the assignment is to practice with your new digital recorders. Find a friend and ask them to tell you a story about something they remember about Link Lake, and record it. We'll talk about it at our next session."

6

Who Has the Money?

If Jackie Jo Jensen heard that bank robbery story once, she heard it twenty-five times since moving to Link Lake after accepting the job as Increase Joseph Memorial Library director. The bank was robbed in 1940. Some folks talk about it as if it happened last week. She heard the most complete version of the story from Fred Russo, a member of the writing class she conducted at the library. The group focused on the history of Link Lake, with the workshop members writing what they remembered about the early days in the community. One day at the library, Fred told Jackie Jo his version of what happened. He said he didn't want to write about it but would tell her the story. He said some of the details were a little sensitive, and several folks in town thought the story should be forgotten rather than discussed continuously or written about.

"The nub of the story is this," Fred said. "The Ames County Bank here in Link Lake was robbed on an October day back in 1940. And somebody here in Link Lake's got the money."

"Is that so?" Jackie Jo said, raising her eyebrows a bit.

"Yup. Somebody right here in town has the loot. No question about it."

"Really?" Jackie Jo was curious about a story she would hear many more times. But none of the stories mentioned the money that Fred included in his version.

"Seems pretty clear that the money is somewhere here in Link Lake. Somebody's got it." Fred hesitated a moment before continuing. "You see this guy, turns out he was a gangster from Chicago, came here on the evening train. Of course, nobody here knew he was a bank robber. In those days, the Chicago Northwestern ran through this town. Half a dozen trains a day. Passenger train coming north in the evening. Passenger train going south in the morning."

Jackie Jo tried to remain interested, but, like so many of the fine citizens of Link Lake, Fred Russo would start a story and then let it wander all over the place before he got to the point.

"Well," Fred continued, "the depot agent was George Willow, name like the tree, and he remembered that this fellow was in his late twenties, early thirties. Good-looking guy. Anyway, he arrived on the evening train. When he asked where he could stay in town, the depot agent remembered telling him that he should walk over to the Williams House, as she had rooms to rent. Miss Phoebe Williams ran the Williams House, also known as a railroad hotel. Wasn't much of a hotel, just a big old house with some extra rooms that Phoebe rented. She had inherited the house from her father, Bill Williams, who had been a lumberman here in town in the early days. Phoebe, who was probably in her mid-thirties in 1940, lived in that big old house all by herself, except for the few roomers who lived there."

Jackie Jo interrupted Fred. "Did you know that I'm staying at the Williams House?"

"Didn't know that," Fred said. "House has quite a history."

"You were talking about some missing money?"

"Well, I'm gettin' to that," Fred said. "You see, this young guy said he lost his job in Chicago and was lookin' for work. Did I tell you his name? Bet I didn't. His name was Adolf Schroeder. Good German name. Lots of German people in Link Lake, you know.

"Well, young Adolf acted like a plain, ordinary single guy lookin' for work. Everybody was lookin' for work in those days. Just gettin' over the Great Depression, we were.

"Did I tell you he was a good-lookin' guy? When he walked down

Main Street, the single girls couldn't help but look his way—married ones looked, too, when their husbands weren't around."

Jackie Jo smiled at the last comment and started moving a pile of books from one place on the checkout counter to another, hoping that Fred would get the hint that she wanted to get back to work.

"Nobody would have guessed that the guy wasn't lookin' for work but was fixing to rob the bank. Imagine that? Adolf Schroeder was a bank robber. He sure pulled the wool over everybody's eyes here in Link Lake. Did I tell you what happened with Miss Phoebe Williams, the mother of the Williams twins who still own the Williams House?" Fred lowered his voice to a whisper, as he knew one of the Williams twins worked at the library and likely was working somewhere in the back.

"No, you didn't," Jackie Jo said, now more than curious about this new twist to the story. She quit stacking books and gave Fred her full attention.

"Well, Miss Phoebe Williams was quite smitten by the young, handsome Adolf Schroeder. Nobody knew about Phoebe and Adolf. But we put two and two together. Nine months after the bank robbery, Phoebe disappeared for a few weeks and returned to the Williams House with twin daughters," Fred said in a near whisper.

"Well, that's quite a story," Jackie Jo said.

"You'll want to keep this story to yourself. The sisters don't talk about it. Can't blame them. Nobody would want it known that their daddy was a bank robber and died in the Waupun Prison. Rumor was that he had hidden the money and promised Phoebe that after serving his time, he'd come back for her and the twins. They'd gather up the money and be gone from Link Lake forever. Course he never returned."

"But what about the money? You said there was still a mystery about the money?"

"I'm just about to tell you that part of the story."

At that moment, a library customer approached the counter to check out a book. Fred said, "I'll see you in writing class next week." He either forgot or decided it was best not to share the rest of the story with Jackie Jo.

Until today, even though she had heard the story several times, the tale obviously had some elements of truth to it. The bank had been robbed, Phoebe Williams did give birth to twin daughters, and Adolf Schroeder had been caught and imprisoned. She never put much stock in the mystery part of the story—what had happened to the money. But that question was surely on the minds of many folks here in Link Lake, especially the old-timers who were here when the bank was robbed.

Jackie Jo had never intended to stay long in Link Lake. She was hoping that this first year would be her last. She searched for open library director positions in one of Wisconsin's larger cities, such as Madison, Eau Claire, or Green Bay. She thought it would be fun to work in Green Bay, as she'd become a Packers fan and had seen how that entire Link Lake community goes bonkers when the Packers are playing.

Sometimes, when the library was not busy, Jackie Jo found herself thinking about the Village of Link Lake, population 1,500. After working in the library for a year, she felt she had a reasonably good idea about the town, its citizens, and the community surrounding it. In her mind, she divided the citizens of Link Lake into two groups. She placed half of the citizens in a group called "The Mostly Contented." For people in this group, as long as their taxes didn't go up, they had a roof over their heads and something to eat, they were mostly happy. People in this group are library customers. They checked out books, contributed to the library's fundraiser bake sales, and used the library's computers, as many couldn't afford their own. They were law-abiding, hardworking, church-attending people. But they feared change, somewhat, but not always, realizing that many of them have experienced some of the most profound changes in the village's history. Many members of this group were stuck in their past. Quite a number of them have trouble setting the bank robbery aside and the mystery of the missing money. Many of them firmly believed the bank robbery money was still in the community, waiting to be found, and like winning the lottery, a reason for getting up in the morning.

Jackie Jo labeled her second group "The Visionary Few," which placed a high value on public tax-supported institutions such as the public library, the local museum, the public schools, the welfare system's food pantry, and used clothing distribution systems. The Visionary Few people were forward-looking. They saw a dark future for Link Lake that "The Mostly Contented" did not see, unless some changes were made.

7

Community Meeting

Before Mayor Jessup opened the meeting at the over-filled community room at the Increase Joseph Memorial Library, he looked around the room. The meeting was scheduled to begin at two o'clock in the afternoon. He noted that former Mayor Olaf Knudson sat in the back of the room, surrounded by several of the former mayor's most vocal supporters. Jessup was well aware that Knudson continued to believe that he, rather than Jessup, should have won the last election. After all, Knudson had been mayor, without opposition, for ten years. He had no love for Mayor Jessup's "off-the-wall ideas," as Knudson described them. And he made sure that everyone within hearing distance would know that. Knudson was also lining up votes for the next election, although it was a couple of years away. Knudson's strategy was to oppose anything and everything that Mayor Jessup suggested, and this meeting was one of the first large gatherings where he hoped to make his position known.

Mayor Jessup spotted Andy Dee, owner and chief announcer for local radio station WLLK-AM, in the back of the room. Mayor Jessup didn't know if Dee was on his side or not. He did know that everyone listened to WLLK-AM, especially to the *Link Lake Voice of Reason*, an hour-long program broadcast at ten o'clock every morning featuring Dee's news for the day, as he saw it. Of course, some people listened mostly to hear his Ole and Ollie stories, which led off his ten o'clock broadcasts. He ended each program with "the old Norwegian says," a bit of philosophy. For most of the broadcast, Dee played polka music, shared the weather every hour, and went off the air at sunset each day to come back on again at sunrise.

"Thank you all for coming out on this rather dreary April day," began Mayor Jessup. "First, I want to thank our head librarian, Ms. Jackie Jo Jensen, for not only helping to set up this meeting but for being of great help to me in planning it. Jackie Jo is with us today.

"Today I want to tell you about two groups that will meet over the next few weeks—each to help do some planning for Link Lake's future. The first: Jackie Jo has a writing class here at the library every Saturday. They are focusing on writing stories about Link Lake's past. She and I agree that a community can't know where it's headed until it knows where it's been."

A few more people continued to crowd into the library's community room as the mayor was talking, standing along the wall by the door. Next, Mayor Jessup said, "I have appointed a Planning Commission to look at Link Lake's current problems and offer some suggestions for solving them. I've asked the commission members to come to this meeting today so I can introduce you to them. Also, if any of you have any suggestions to help us solve some of Link Lake's problems, get in touch with me or one of the commission members.

"I will be holding several community meetings to bring you up-to-date with what the Planning Commission is discussing and also hear a story or two from Jackie Jo's writing class.

"So here are the members of the Planning Commission. Let's start with you, Tony."

A tall, thin, twenty-something young man with a small ring in one ear and wearing his long hair in a ponytail stood up. "Well, I'm Tony Noble, and I'm a graduate student at the University of Wisconsin–Oshkosh. I grew up here in Link Lake, and my folks still live here—some of you likely know them, Bill and Eleanor Noble. My dad's retired now, but he worked at the lumberyard for many years."

"Thanks for agreeing to be a part of our group, Tony," said Jon.

A VILLAGE LOOKS AHEAD

"No problem."

"Robert, you're next," said the mayor

"I'm Robert Spranger," said a middle-aged man with graying sideburns and carrying a few extra pounds. "As most of you know, I own Spranger Hardware here in Link Lake. My dad, Louie Spranger, owned the place before me."

"Glad to have you with us," said the mayor as he nodded to the next person.

"I'm Gwen Jones," said an older, white-haired woman who wore glasses that sat on the end of her nose. She was "thin as a post," as some people in Link Lake described her. "I retired from UW–Madison, where I taught rural sociology. I moved to Link Lake a few years ago."

"Thanks, Gwen," said Jon as he turned to the next person sitting in the front row.

"I'm Oscar Anderson. I'm a retired farmer, and I'm pleased to be a part of this commission."

"Okay, here's what I would like the Planning Commission to do," began Jon. "As you know, we have many towns about the size of Link Lake scattered all across the Midwest, with around one thousand citizens, more or less. And many of these towns are not doing well."

Gwen Jones held up her hand.

"Let me tell you how they are not doing well and why. Roads need repair. There is little to no high-speed internet. Yes, I work on a computer. Rural schools are suffering from a lack of resources. Our taxes are reasonable, but the wages in this area are low, and besides that, jobs are scarce. When young people graduate from high school in a rural community, they leave and never come back. They find jobs in Milwaukee, in Madison, in the Fox River Valley. One of the reasons we are not doing well is that most of the state's resources go to Madison and Milwaukee, and those of us in the hinterland, as we are sometimes called, are left behind." Gwen stopped to take a breath.

"Gwen, I don't think many people in Link Lake would argue with you. Link Lake and villages like ours are suffering, some more than others. This is especially so since the Great Recession back in 2007–

2009. That's why I appointed the Planning Commission—to develop a plan for Link Lake's future. To not wait to see what happens and then respond to it, but to take the future by the neck and shake it so we get our fair share and have our future what we want it to be, not what somebody else thinks it should be."

"Seems a bit hopeless," said Robert. "These days are nothing like the good old days when Link Lake was booming. Some days only a handful of people stop in my hardware store."

"Robert, I know lots of folks in Link Lake would like to return to the past. I hear that almost every day. But I don't think it will happen. I do think we can learn from the past. In fact, we must. I once heard a speaker say, 'When we forget our histories, we forget who we are.' I fully believe that. I'm pleased that the Link Lake writers class is wrestling with that very question, re-discovering our history and then writing it down. Our group can learn from them. But the mission of this group is to look ahead and do some crystal balling about the kind of future we'd like."

8
Radio WLLK

"This is radio station WLLK-AM, *The Voice of Reason* here in Link Lake, Wisconsin. I'm your host, Andy Dee. It's ten o'clock and a beautiful morning in our beautiful village. You are probably wondering what's been going on with Ole and Ollie. It seems they went fishing over in Norwegian Lake the other day. They rented a boat, rowed out to the middle of the lake, and dropped in their lines. Soon they were catching big bluegills, one right after the other. They couldn't believe their luck in finding this great fishing place.

"Ole said, 'It's too bad we don't have some paint with us.'

"'What would you do with paint?' answered Ollie.

"'I'd paint a big X in the bottom of the boat so we could find this place again,' said Ollie.

"Ole laughed. 'Ollie, that wouldn't work. Next time we'll probably have a different boat.'

"So, we'll leave Ole and Ollie and turn to the news of the day. First the weather report. Low temperature this morning, forty degrees, high of fifty-five by mid-afternoon. Some clouds. No rain. Probably could use some rain. The sandy soil of Ames County always needs rain, it seems.

"I have some news to report. Mayor Jessup held an all-community meeting at the community room at the Link Lake Library. He told of his plans to help the Village of Link Lake look at itself and make plans for the future. He told us about the writing class that Jackie Jo is teaching at the library and introduced us to his newly formed Planning Commission, which will look at Link Lake's problems and offer solutions. I'm thinking our town could use a few new ideas. People don't like to hear this, but my take on Link Lake is that it has been treading water for a couple of decades. To take this swimming example a bit further, even good swimmers eventually have to swim to shore or they drown. Which is it for Link Lake? I'll sit in on as many of the mayor's commission meetings and report on their discussion. I'll keep you up-to-date as I learn more about the commission's discussions and the history work the library's writing class is coming up with."

After completing a recent *Voice of Reason* segment, which he did six days a week, Andy Dee thought about how the radio station, which he now owns, got started. Andy Dee's father first opened WLLK-AM back in 1970. He called himself Freddy Dee. Today, many years later, Dee wondered if anybody knew that his dad's real name was Anders Dahl and that he was a Norwegian kid who had left the Dahl farm when he graduated from Link Lake High School and "buggered off" to Madison and the big university there (that's how his dad, Anders, had described his leaving the farm). This was back in the 1960s when the Vietnam War was raging. Dahl was colorblind. Thus, he avoided the draft that was scooping up young men from across the country. While at the university, young Dahl got caught up in the protests against the war. He let his blond hair grow until it touched his shoulders. He marched with the protestors and attended massive rallies. Mr. and Mrs. Dahl, back on the home farm just out of Link Lake, weren't very pleased to learn "what that damn university had done to their son," as Mr. Dahl described the situation one day while he waited for his grist at the Link Lake gristmill.

One thing he learned how to do while at the university when he wasn't protesting or studying—he was actually quite a good student— was to begin playing poker with a few of his friends. He soon became an outstanding poker player, playing in national poker tournaments in Las Vegas and making lots of money. He never told anyone, especially his parents, that he had earned more money in a single poker tournament than they had made in a year from their farm. One of his favorite courses at the UW had been a radio communications course, where he learned the rudiments of doing radio programs, which earned him a spot as an announcer on the campus radio station. In addition, because he was curious, he learned what to do in front of a microphone and what happened on the other side—he learned the engineering side of radio work.

He knew what he wanted to do when he graduated from the UW with a degree in agricultural journalism. He wanted to start a radio station in his hometown of Link Lake, Wisconsin. And that's what he did. He never told anyone where he had gotten his money to do that, other than once saying that a wealthy benefactor was financing his operation. No one ever knew that WLLK-AM, *The Voice of Reason*, was financed from poker earnings.

Today the old Norwegian says: "When it's over, it's often not over, except when it is."

9
Fred and Oscar

Fred Russo and Oscar Anderson arrived at the same time for their regular Monday morning coffee chat at the café and shuffled their way through the morning customers to their reserved table. They were neighbors and could very well drive into Link Lake together, but driving their pickups—Fred had a Ford, and Oscar a Chevrolet—was one way they expressed their independence.

"Well, Oscar," said Fred. "See you made it on time today."

"Me make it on time, Fred? You know damn well that it's you that's usually late. By the way, did you git yourself a new alarm clock?"

"I didn't get no new alarm clock. I got important things to do. And when I've got important things to do, I'm on time, sometimes a little early."

"Well, you weren't a little early today," said Oscar.

"Oscar, I've got important stuff to talk about, and I don't wanna waste my breath talkin' about how early or late I am."

"Morning, boys," said Pauline, who arrived at their table carrying two empty cups and a coffee pot. "How you doin' this morning?" she said as she placed a cup in front of each of them and filled it with coffee.

"Feeling better than I should for a guy my age," offered Oscar.

Pauline smiled. "You guys want one of our big caramel rolls? We popped them out of the oven no more than ten minutes ago."

"Sounds good, but I don't need any more pounds," said Fred.

"Gotta take a pass as well," said Oscar. "I can smell 'em way over here, though. Sure smell good."

"So what's new with you, Fred?" asked Oscar as he took a big swig of coffee.

"Lots of stuff, Oscar. Lots of stuff."

"Such as?" asked Oscar, remembering that he had put his old friend on the list of candidates for the writer's workshop at the library.

"Well, we had our first meeting at the library last Saturday," said Fred. "And you're right. That new librarian, Jackie, is something, quite a looker. Course I'm old enough to be her grandfather."

"So what'd you do, just sit there and stare at the librarian?"

"I did not just sit there and stare at the librarian," Fred said, a bit exasperated with his old friend. "Miss Jackie, by the way, she's a heckuva good teacher. She started showing how to get in touch with our memories when we were kids and write down a story about them."

"So, what'd you remember? Was a long time since you were a kid, Fred."

Fred touched his finger to his head. "Lots of memories up here, Oscar. Lots of memories. They ain't going no place. They're still up here. Surprised myself that I did."

"So, what'd you remember that's got you so dang excited?"

"Well, Miss Jackie Jo asked us to remember our favorite toy when we were kids."

"Favorite toy, huh?" Oscar said, trying to keep a serious look on his face.

"Yup, favorite toy. And you know what I remembered, Oscar? You know what I remembered?"

"How in the hell should I know what your favorite toy was when you were a kid?"

"Well, I'll tell you what it was. It was a little black horse made out of cast iron. I remember how Pa helped me make a little harness for it out of store string. I must have been only three years old at the time."

"You remember something when you were three?" asked Oscar.

"Well, maybe I was three and a half. Anyway, that was one fine little horse. I still have it. Sits on the clock shelf. Only has three legs. One got busted off, but I don't remember how it happened. But I still got that little horse. You bet I do," said Fred. He had a faraway look on his face.

Pauline came by with coffee refills, which both old men readily accepted.

"So what was your favorite toy when you were a kid?" Fred asked after taking another sip of coffee.

"A teddy bear," Oscar said quietly.

"An old store-bought teddy bear?"

"Wasn't store-bought."

"How'd you know?"

"'Cause my ma made it."

"Made it? How'd your ma make a teddy bear?" Fred had a puzzled look on his face as he looked around to see if any of the morning coffee drinkers at the Black Oak were listening in on their conversation about kids' toys. None appeared interested.

"Well, the teddy bear, front and back, came printed on a flour sack that Ma bought. I think she bought it 'cause she saw the makin's of the little bear. Once the flour was dumped from the sack, she cut out the bear's front and back and sewed 'em together. Then she filled the little bear with quilt stuffin', the same material she used when making a quilt. Made the nicest little bear. I carried it with me everywhere I went."

"You still got that teddy bear, like I got my little three-legged iron horse?" asked Fred.

"Nope, I don't. But I got the memory. Nobody can take the memory away—unless I come down with that old-timer's disease that steals people's memories and rots their brains."

Both old men sat quietly for a few moments, pondering people they knew who were losing their memories because of various kinds of dementia.

"So what else is your writing group doing?" asked Oscar.

"We're doin' some important stuff. Mayor Jessup even stopped to talk with us. Imagine that. Our writing group is important enough that the mayor would stop by."

"So what'd the mayor have to say?" Oscar held back what the Planning Commission had been talking about.

"Well, one thing he did was give us each something. I got it right here in my pocket." Fred retrieved the little recorder from his pocket.

"What's that? Looks like a cigarette lighter."

"Oscar, it's no damn cigarette lighter. Don't know if they even make cigarette lighters anymore."

"So what is it?"

"Anybody who's with it has knowledge about what's going on in the world knows that this is a digital recorder." He handed the recorder to Oscar to inspect.

"Well, Mr. well-informed and up-to-date on what's happening in the world, what are you planning to do with a digital recorder? Sure not much to it, is there?"

"The mayor gave each of us one of these and asked us to record stories that old-timers in our community might share with us. So, we're doin' two things. We're writing down our own stories, and we're movin' out in the community and recording other people's stories."

"So who are you gonna interview, Fred?" Oscar asked.

"To start with, I'm thinkin' about interviewing you."

"Me? Why me?"

"'Cause you and me know what farmin' was like before it changed. Before it got to be so damn complicated that it's hard to figure out just what it is these days. Do some thinkin' about the early days, Oscar. And maybe next week, I can stop by your place and put this little recorder to work."

"Well, that's quite a report," Oscar said. "I've got some news, too. As you know, I sit on the mayor's Planning Commission. Two big things we've been discussing: how Link Lake can make its own electricity and how it can better provide fresh food for all of us."

"Really? Those are pretty big ideas. Lots of people still have home gardens, but gardens pretty much go to sleep from October to May," said Fred.

"That they do, but guess what is coming to Link Lake?"

"What?" asked Fred.

"A company that is going to build several greenhouses so we can have fresh vegetables all year round."

"Really," said Fred.

"Yup," said Oscar. "They will have a store at the greenhouse where you can buy the vegetables. They will also work with the local restaurants so they can have fresh vegetables all year-round as well."

"You gonna tell me what vegetables they'd grow in these greenhouses?" said Oscar.

"Yes, here's the list by season: spring—lettuce, peas, onions; summer—cucumbers, squash, peppers, tomatoes, beans, carrots; late fall and winter—carrots, rutabagas, beets, potatoes, brussels sprouts."

10
Dexter Comes to Town

On the following Friday afternoon, Jackie Jo met the bus in Willow River. She was looking forward to seeing her boyfriend Dexter, spending the weekend with him, or at least part of the weekend, as she had the writing class to teach on Saturday morning—the group had changed the time from afternoon to morning. "Lot sharper in the morning," Fred Russo had mentioned to Jackie Jo when she asked about the time they should meet next.

Dexter stepped off the bus, which stopped at the Shell gas station in Willow River, and immediately saw a smiling Jackie Jo standing near her car. He slung his backpack over his shoulder, rushed over, and gave Jackie Jo a big hug and kiss. Dexter had long black hair and was about six feet tall. He was thin as a steel fence post and wore a black stud in each ear.

"So good to see you, kiddo, and just where am I?" Dexter said, looking around.

"You are in Willow River, Wisconsin," said Jackie Jo. She took Dexter's hand and walked him toward her car.

"So where is Link Lake? And how come the bus doesn't go there?"

"Link Lake is eight miles down the road. And I have no idea why the bus doesn't go there," said Jackie Jo.

"So good to see you, Dex. I've missed you. Missed you a lot."

"Well, I'm glad I am missed. Never been this far north before. How far are we from Upper Michigan?"

"You ever look at a map, Dex? We are a long way from Upper Michigan, and we really are not north. This is central Wisconsin."

They began driving along Highway 22 toward Link Lake. "This really looks like the boonies," said Dexter as they drove several miles through pine plantations that lined both sides of the road. "Does anybody live here? All I see is trees."

Jackie Jo laughed. "Yes, people live here, Dex, but this is not Chicago, or Milwaukee, or Madison."

As they neared Link Lake, Jackie Jo pointed out the lake. "We're almost there. See the lake in the distance? It's called Link Lake, same name as the village. I haven't had time to do much exploring yet."

"Do they have any restaurants in Hicksville?" asked Dexter.

"They do. And the town is Link Lake. You'll not make any friends giving the town derogatory names."

"I'm not so sure I'd want any friends in this backward place."

"Dex, the place is not backward; it may look that way to guys like you. But it has very progressive thinking people."

"I'll bet," said Dexter. "Where's this restaurant you mentioned? I'm starved."

"It's called the Black Oak Café, and it's located right on Main Street. I've eaten there several times."

"Food any good?"

"It's good food. Nothing fancy. Just good country food."

"As compared to city food?"

"Dexter, try and be nice."

"I'll try, but I think it's going to be a challenge."

They parked in front of the Black Oak, and although the place was almost filled, they spotted an empty table near the back.

"Wow, this is like being in some kind of wildlife museum." He glanced at the mounted deer head displayed above the door, the mounted fish on the wall behind the cash register, and something big and black fastened to the far wall.

"What is that?" asked Dexter, pointing to the black something. He said it loud enough that a few heads turned when they overheard his question.

"Oh, that's a bearskin," Jackie Jo said nonchalantly. She remembered asking the same question the first time she ate here.

"Wow," Dexter said again. "I've never been in a place like this before."

"Dex, you've spent too much time in a city."

"Place is nearly filled with people," said Dexter.

"It's Friday night, and Friday night is fish fry night. Everybody eats fish on Friday night."

"Strange," said Dexter as he picked up a menu and began studying it.

"Fish specials are written on the blackboard," Jackie Jo said, pointing to the list:

> *Fish Fry: $6.95 Includes salad bar and choice of potato*
> *Baked Cod: $7.95 Includes salad bar and choice of potato*

"Hi, Jackie," said Pauline, who had two empty cups in her hand and a coffee pot. "Can I pour you some coffee?"

"Sure," said Jackie Jo. "Pauline, this is my friend Dexter. He is visiting this weekend."

"Welcome to Link Lake, Dexter. Always nice to see new faces in Link Lake, especially in the winter. Where do you live?"

"In Madison."

"Welcome to the north," Pauline said with a big smile. She used this line when talking with newcomers and learned they were from southern Wisconsin or Illinois.

"I'll be back in a minute to take your order," Pauline said as she walked to the table near them and filled coffee cups.

"It's my treat," said Jackie Jo. "And I'm having the fish fry."

"Isn't that loaded with calories?"

"Probably, but the fish really tastes good, and the salad bar is better than anything I remember in Madison. Besides, Dex you are skinny as a rail, as people around here would describe you. A few extra calories won't make a difference."

"Okay. I'll give it a try," said Dexter.

With their meal nearly finished and Dexter confessing that Jackie Jo was right about both the quality of the salad bar and how well the fish tasted, he asked, "So what's there to do here in Link Lake in the middle of winter?" asked Dexter.

"Well, tomorrow morning, I'm leading a writing class. And you are welcome to sit in," said Jackie Jo.

"That sounds exciting," grumbled Dexter.

"It really is. I've never taught anything before, and I must say, it's kind of fun working with a group of older people."

"How old?"

"Oh, sixties, seventies, eighties." Jackie Jo smiled.

"Geez, they're ancient. How can a bunch of old geezers write anything?"

"You'd be surprised, Dex. Come along with me, and you'll see. I've also got a fun activity planned for us on Saturday afternoon."

"And what would that be? It's pretty darn cold out, you know."

"It's a secret, Dex," she said, putting her hand on his arm.

"The only thing I can tell you is lots of folks around here do it."

Jackie Jo had reserved a room for Dexter at the Williams House, and after the two of them had breakfast at the Black Oak the following morning, they walked to the library, where several of the writing class members were already waiting to get in.

Jackie Jo introduced Dexter to the group and said he was a friend visiting from Madison and would sit in on the class. What really happened was that Dexter sat in the back reading a book and not paying much attention to what the class was doing. He was thinking about what surprise activity she had planned for them in the afternoon.

With the morning workshop concluded and a quick lunch, Jackie Jo and Dexter returned to the Williams House. Jackie Jo suggested that Dexter put on warm clothing because what she had planned required warm clothing.

"Okay," said Jackie Jo. "We're off on our afternoon adventure." They got into Jackie's car and drove the short distance to the boat landing at the frozen Link Lake. There they met Fred Russo, who was waiting in his pickup at the landing.

"Hi, Fred," Jackie Jo said. "You remember Dexter from this morning?"

"Yup, I do. You ever do any ice fishing?"

"Ice fishing? You mean catching fish through the ice?"

"Yup, that's about it," said Fred.

"It's my surprise," said Jackie Jo. "Should be fun."

"Fishing through the ice is fun?" muttered Dexter under his breath.

"Have the two of you got fishing licenses?"

"No . . ." said Jackie Jo. "Haven't thought about that."

"All you need to do is march right over there to Ted's Bait Shop." Fred pointed to a little building a few yards from the boat landing. "Ted'll fix you up with licenses. I've got all the equipment and bait we'll need."

With their new fishing licenses in hand, Jackie Jo and Dexter, with Fred in the lead, set off across Link Lake toward a little ice fishing shack that Fred had pointed out. They saw a village of ice fishing shacks, all about the same size, all with runners under them so they could be pulled over the ice.

"Oscar Anderson is in the shack waiting for us," said Fred. "He said he met you the first week you were in town."

"I remember," said Jackie, pulling her wool cap down farther over her head as the trio walked into a brisk northwest wind.

Dexter said nothing as he walked with his head down and his hands over his ears, trying to keep them warm.

"Well, here we are," said Fred. "This is the Fred-Oscar Lair. Has quite a reputation here on Link Lake, if I must say so myself."

Fred knocked on the door. "You in there, Oscar?" He knew he was because he could see the thread of smoke coming from the shanty's little stove.

"Come in, come in," said Oscar. "Great day for ice fishing, although I haven't had any bites yet."

"You remember Jackie, our new librarian," said Fred. "This is her friend, Dexter. Neither of them has been ice fishing."

"Well, it's high time you learned how," said Oscar, chuckling. "Find a place to sit, and be careful you don't step in a fish hole and end up with a wet foot."

Once in the shack, Dexter immediately began rubbing his hands over the little woodstove in one corner. "Geez, it's cold out there."

"Not bad today. I was here last year when it got down to twenty below. Now twenty below starts to be cold," Oscar chuckled.

Oscar showed Jackie Jo and Dexter how to thread a little wax worm onto their fish hooks. He had a little box of pale, wiggly worms about a quarter-inch long. Fred and Jackie Jo huddled over one of the holes, Oscar and Dexter over the other, each watching a tiny red bobber attached to the thin monofilament line.

"So how are you liking Link Lake so far?" asked Fred.

"Good food at the Black Oak," said Dexter, not wanting to say that people going ice fishing was about the dumbest thing he'd heard anyone doing.

"What's happening?" said Jackie, excited to see her bobber dive nearly out of sight.

"You've got a bite," said Oscar. "Set the hook and pull 'em in."

Jackie Jo lifted the pole, and soon a fat bluegill was flopping on the floor of the shanty.

"Dex, look at this. I caught a fish. I caught a fish," Jackie Jo said excitedly.

"I see that," said Dexter, not sounding at all impressed.

The foursome sat staring at their red bobbers for the rest of the afternoon as Oscar occasionally stuffed another stick of oak wood into the stove.

"Wanna snort of this?" Oscar said as he dug a bottle out of his coat pocket and handed it to Dexter.

"What is it?"

"Wine. Made it myself. It's grape wine made from wild grapes. Grow hair on your chest."

"No thanks," said Dexter, who continued to wonder about this place that was beginning to look like it was right out of the nineteenth century. Fishing through the ice on a cold winter day. Drinking homemade wine right out of the bottle.

Oscar took a big swig of the wine and passed to bottle to Fred, who did likewise.

"How about you, Miss Jackie? You wanna swig? Warm you up."

"No thanks, but thanks for offering," Jackie Jo said, watching her hole, waiting to see if another bluegill might take her line.

11
Break Up

Arriving five minutes after the library opened, Ethyl Williams, who was never late, greeted Jackie Jo. "Are you not well?" Ethyl asked.

"I'm . . . I'm okay."

"You don't sound okay, and you don't look okay."

"Not a good weekend," murmured Jackie Jo.

"Something happen at your Saturday writing class? Somebody give you a hard time? Was it the preacher? He can come on pretty strong sometimes. Or Emily? She can be pretty blustery. Was it one of them?"

"Nobody gave me a hard time at the writing class. In fact, it went pretty well." Jackie Jo found her handkerchief and wiped her eyes.

"Child, you are crying," said Ethyl. "What's wrong?"

"My boyfriend visited this weekend. Dexter's his name."

"That should have been fun."

"Dexter and I went fishing with Fred Russo and Oscar Anderson on the lake."

"Those guys are great old ice fishermen. They do a lot of it every winter," offered Ethyl. "You catch any fish?"

"Caught one, a bluegill—that's what Fred called it."

Jackie Jo began sobbing, and Ethyl put her arm around her.

"So what went wrong?"

"Dexter and I broke up. That's what went wrong," Jackie Jo sobbed.

"Why?" was all Ethyl could think to ask.

"It's a long story."

"I've got time. The books can wait."

"It started back when I first accepted this job as librarian. Dexter thought it was the dumbest thing I ever did to accept a job in 'backwater Link Lake.' Those were his very words." Jackie Jo wiped her eyes again. "And starting Friday, when I picked him up from the bus in Willow River until I dumped him off at the bus station yesterday, all he could do was make fun of this place. He made fun of the Black Oak Café. He thought my writing class was dumb—he sat in on it. And then," Jackie Jo began sobbing again, "I thought it was great that Fred asked us to go ice fishing with Oscar and him. Thought he'd find it at least interesting. He said it was primitive and a throwback to the 1800s. What a jerk."

Ethyl said nothing.

"I tried to explain to him that Link Lake was similar to many central and northern Wisconsin villages struggling with their futures and trying to adjust to the many changes they have seen in the past fifty years. I told him about Mayor Jessup's group that was looking at future directions. I tried to tell him about the importance of my writing class and how a community needs to know where it's been as it examines its future. He laughed. 'Nobody cares about the past. It's the future that's important,' he said."

"Sounds like Dexter needs to spend more time in the country," said Ethyl.

"His mind is made up. He thinks rural people are lazy, that they spend too much time fishing and not enough time working. I told him that Oscar and Fred were in their eighties and deserved to enjoy not working. He said there was no hope for these little communities, that the country would be better off if they just disappeared. Then he said, 'We all know the future of this country is in the urban areas. The writing is on the wall.'" Jackie Jo began sobbing again.

"There are people like that. Too many, I'm afraid, that simply don't understand what it's like to live in the country or in a small town like Link Lake," said Ethyl, shaking her head.

"You know what was the last straw?" asked Jackie Jo.

"I surely wouldn't know," said Ethyl.

"He said that if I kept working here in this dumb little forgotten town, I should forget about any relationship with him. That's what he said, the jerk." The tears began flowing down Jackie Jo's cheeks again. "I said, 'Have it your way and have a good life.' I hope I never see him again."

"Why don't you go to your office and work there for a while this morning? I'll take care of the library customers," said Ethyl.

"Thank you, Ethyl. Sorry to dump all of this on you."

12

Fred and Oscar

The two old farmers arrived at the Black Oak Café within two minutes of each other. Neither wanted to be accused of being late. Being late appeared to be a mortal sin for these old retired farmers. They tossed their caps on an empty chair, hung their jackets on the back of their chairs, and sat down, neither saying anything as they sipped coffee that Pauline had recently poured.

Oscar scratched his chin and finally said, "Mornin', Fred."

"Mornin'," Fred said, taking another sip of coffee.

"So what's new?" asked Oscar.

"Not much. Except one of my barn cats came up missing this morning. An old cat he is. Named him Thunder. Good mouser too. Scarcely a day goes by when I don't see him comin' into the barn carrying a dead mouse in his mouth. Wonder what happened to him. He is an explorer—turned up once at Bill Miller's place, a half mile down the road. Maybe that's where he went today."

The two old farmers sat quietly again, eating the fried eggs and toast Pauline had recently brought to their tables.

"So what'd you think of Jackie Jo's boyfriend?" asked Oscar quietly.

Fred didn't say anything for a half minute or so, then said, "First thing I noticed was that he was so damn skinny a strong wind would pick him up and move him to the next county. Can't remember when

I saw somebody so thin. I'm guessing where he comes from they don't have much to eat."

"Can't argue about that. He was one of the skinniest buggers I've ever seen," said Oscar. "Anything else about him?"

"He's got what looks like a bad bruise on his right wrist," Fred offered.

Oscar laughed. "Fred, that ain't no bruise. That's a tattoo. Tattoo of a compass."

"Compass, huh? I thought a compass was used to find direction. This guy lost all the time, so he needs a compass right on his wrist?" Fred said.

"That ain't no real compass, just a picture of one. Kind of a decoration."

"Oh," said Fred. "Seems kinda dumb to me. Saw something else I couldn't figure out, but I didn't say anything."

"And that would be?" asked Oscar, smiling as he took another sip of his coffee.

"Guy's got something stuck to each of his earlobes. Never saw nothin' like that before," said Fred, chasing a last piece of fried egg around his plate. "Somethin' black and the size of a paper eraser. Maybe was a paper eraser. Couldn't really tell."

Oscar laughed. "That's no paper eraser. It's an earring. Some men wear them these days."

"Well, I'll be damned. An earring. I thought they were for women—never heard that men wore them," said Fred. "Learn something new every day. Sort of wished I hadn't learned about this earring thing. Just don't seem right." Fred shook his head.

The two farmers continued to finish their breakfast without talking. Finally, Fred broke the silence, "Whadda think the boyfriend thought about ice fishing?" Fred asked quietly.

"He hated it," Oscar said. "I was watching him. Once we got his line in the water and bobber floatin', I don't think he looked at it once. Jackie Jo seemed to be having a good time. About all he did was sit by the stove and rub his hands together. That's what he did the entire time we were there. Didn't say a word. Not one damn word.

A VILLAGE LOOKS AHEAD

Somethin's really wrong with that guy."

"That's my take, too. Wonder what in the world Jackie Jo sees in that guy—she ain't nothin' like him. Nothin' at all," said Fred.

13
Writing Class

The following Saturday, the writing class met once more. Several of them had little stories they wrote when they were twelve years old, which had been their assignment for the week. Fred wondered if Jackie Jo would say anything about her ice fishing experience with Oscar, her boyfriend, and him. But she didn't mention it.

"Anyone want to share the story they wrote when they were twelve years old?" Fred raised his hand.

"Thank you, Fred. Go right ahead," Jackie Jo said, smiling as she had come to like and appreciate Fred.

"Well," Fred began, as he cleared his throat and unfolded a piece of paper with scribbling on it. "I ain't much for writing, but I've got lots of stories." Fred began as he adjusted his glasses and held up the single sheet of paper.

"When I was twelve years old, I was a member of the Link Lake 4-H club. I was a farm kid, and all the farm kids around Link Lake belonged. The summer I was twelve, I had a bull calf for a 4-H project. Named him Thunder. Those who know farming and bull calves know that a bull calf can be quite a handful. They are strong-minded and bull-headed." Fred stopped to chuckle at his attempt at humor.

"All of us 4-H kids in the dairy project looked forward to showing our calves at the county fair. To do that, we had to teach our calves how to lead with a short rope. All summer long, when I wasn't doing work on the farm, I worked at teaching Thunder how to lead. Some times I wanted to quit doing it. I thought I was making progress, then there was no progress at all. Pa said I must keep at it, 'Farm kids are not quitters,' he said. So I continued. Some days I couldn't get Thunder to move. He wouldn't take a step. Just stood there, all four legs planted on the ground and shaking his head at me. Other days, he'd take off running, dragging me along behind him. It weren't no fun at all. I wasn't so sure I wanted to take him to the fair. But Pa said, 'Thunder will be just fine when you get him to the fair.' I wasn't at all sure Pa was right, but I learned a long time ago not to argue with Pa.

"August and fair time rolled around. I both looked forward to the fair where we dairy 4-H boys got to stay overnight and dreaded what Thunder would do once I got him in the show ring with a bunch of other bull calves. I couldn't imagine what I'd do if he began acting up in front of the cattle judge and all the people watching the judging.

"On Thursday, the entry day for the Ames County Fair, George Wilkins, the community livestock trucker, stopped by our farm to pick up my calf. Thunder walked into the truck as if he had done it many times before, which he obviously had not done. I relaxed a bit. Maybe I've been worrying too much about Thunder's behavior. He seemed all relaxed and looking forward to what was coming next.

"Pa and I met the trucker at the fairgrounds and helped him unload Thunder. No problem at all. He walked down the truck's loading ramp like he'd done it every day. I led him into the fair's calf barn and tied him to the manager that was there to feed him hay. We'd brought a couple of sacks of hay with us so Thunder would have plenty to eat while he was at the fair. I rubbed Thunder's head, which he liked me to do, and said I would see him later. Pa told me everything looked okay, and he said he had to head home to do chores and he would see me tomorrow. I saw a couple of the boys from our 4-H club, and we walked down the midway toward where they had pitched our sleeping tent. The 4-H club bought a surplus army tent for this purpose.

"The fair was the highlight for me every year while I was in 4-H. I so much enjoyed the smells—the barn smells that reminded me of home mixed with the smells of onions and hamburgers frying coming from the various food sellers. And the farm sounds coming from the barns, calves bellowing, turkeys calling, ducks quacking, roosters crowing, mixed with the sounds of the midway rides: the merry-go-round, the Tilt-a-Whirl, and the Ferris wheel.

"I can't say enough about how fun it was sleeping with the other 4-H boys in the old army tent. I fell sound asleep once I had climbed onto my surplus army cot. Before I knew it, it was five o'clock in the morning, and our 4-H leader, Clayton Owens, who had spent the night with us in the tent, was waking us up and telling us it was time to tend to our 4-H calves.

"The other sleepy boys and I walked across the dark and quiet midway to the cattle barn, where Thunder had spent the night. When I saw him, I gave him a big hug and took some hay from the hay sack and put it in front of him. Then I began brushing him and cleaning his hoofs and horns in preparation for the show ring competition, which began at eight. Pa arrived from home a little before eight to help me put the final touches on Thunder before I led him into the show ring. Thunder didn't look the least bit anxious; I was scared to death.

"Promptly at eight, our judging class was called. I untied Thunder from the stall, clipped the lead rope to his halter, and led him out to the show ring. I walked around the show ring with a fellow competitor behind me and another in front of me. A few of the little bull calves were jumping around a bit and not wanting to walk slowly with their heads up by the judge. But not Thunder. He did everything I asked him to do—no jumping around, no showing off. The show ring was enclosed with snow fence about four feet tall, with a little gate on one end. The cattle judge stood in the middle of the show ring. As each of us walked by the judge, he looked carefully at each calf—he had a most serious look on his face.

"And then it happened. *Kaboom!* It sounded like a rifle shot. I learned later it had been one of those giant firecrackers a kid set off as a prank to see how the calves would react.

"Upon hearing the loud noise, Thunder jumped with all four feet into the air, and then he took off for the show ring gate at a gallop, with me hanging onto the lead rope and trying to keep up. Upon reaching the gate, I tripped and fell, and Thunder galloped down the midway with the lead rope dragging behind him. I heard someone on the midway yell, 'Look out. There's a wild cow coming this way.' I thought, *What a dummy. The person can't tell a cow from a bull calf.*

"I got up, brushed myself off, and began running after my calf, who was now some distance ahead of me as it ran down the midway, scattering the carnie workers who were not accustomed to seeing runaway calves in their midst.

"Thunder had stopped running when he reached the high fence at the south end of the fairgrounds. When I got to him, I saw two little girls, musta been no more than two or three years rubbin' Thunder's head. He seemed to be enjoying every minute of the attention.

"I thanked the little girls for taking good care of my calf and led Thunder down the midway as the carnie workers watched but didn't say a word. Arriving at the show ring, I noticed that the judge was just finishing judging the little bulls. I led Thunder into the show ring and the judge handed me a pink ribbon, fourth place and last in the class. Pa was there, and he put his big hand on my shoulder. 'Next time we'll do better,' he said."

Fred folded up his several sheets of paper and put them aside. His fellow writing classmates began clapping. "Well done," Jackie Jo said. "Can I give your story to the mayor to share with his Planning Commission?"

"Sure," Fred said, smiling broadly.

Jackie Jo and the other writing group members listened as other members shared their brief stories of memories when they were twelve years old. Jackie Jo had also asked Emily Higgins, president of the historical society, if she would do some digging into the early history of Link Lake, when it got started, how it got its name, and so on. She agreed to do it.

14
Community Meeting

It was a warm Saturday afternoon when Mayor Jessup invited the Link Lake community and those folks living around it to meet once more to get an update on the Planning Commission's activities. They met in the library's community room, where they had met previously. The room was filled to capacity, as it was at the previous meeting. Once more, former Mayor Olaf Knudson sat with a dozen or so of his most loyal followers in the back of the room, listening and taking notes but mostly remaining quiet.

"Thank you all for coming out on this beautiful day in Link Lake," began the mayor. "As I've mentioned previously, we have two groups in Link Lake. One is discussing where we have been, the other is focused on where we should be headed. I have a treat for you today. Jackie Jo, our librarian, has asked her writing class to write stories about something they remember when they were twelve years old and growing up in the Link Lake community. Fred Russo, a retired farmer who many of you know, wrote a piece about when he was a 4-H member showing calves at the Ames County Fair. The Russo Farm, where Fred grew up and still lives, is just a mile or so out of town. Jackie Jo showed the story to me, and I invited Fred to read his story to you today. By the way, how many of you were 4-H members at one time or another?" About half of the group raised their hands.

Fred, wearing what looked to be new bib overalls, slowly made his way to the podium. Once there, he reached into his pocket and removed several sheets of paper covered with handwriting. He unfolded the first wrinkled sheet, looked out over the audience, and began with a clear, strong voice.

"I'm Fred Russo. I spent my life farming, and I've done little or no writing. I also didn't much care for standing in front of a group and talking. This was Jackie Jo, the librarian's idea, and I'm doing this as a favor to her. I've titled my little piece, 'Living with Thunder,' the name of my 4-H calf when I was twelve years old."

Fred began reading his story about Thunder, his 4-H calf, the trouble he had teaching him how to lead, and his problems when he took him to the fair, and the calf was frightened and ran away. When he finished reading, he folded the wrinkled sheets of paper and stuffed them into his bib overall pockets. He smiled as he listened to the considerable applause that came from the audience. Several people shook his hand as he shuffled back to his seat.

Mayor Jon Jessup returned to the podium and said, "Fred, that was just great. Many of us have memories of the county fair. Let's give Fred another round of applause." Mayor Jessup continued, "Let's not forget that the Ames County Fair is still going strong. If you haven't stopped by the fair recently, you want to do it. It's the third weekend in August each year.

"Changing the subject a bit, you all know that our Planning Commission, working with the writers' class at the library, is searching for ways to give our little community a boost. To bring it into the twenty-first century. As we do that, we on the Planning Commission have all agreed that whatever we do, we must do it without harming the environment." The mayor purposely looked to where the previous mayor and his group of admirers sat, all shaking their heads no.

"I know that some of you don't agree with what we are doing," the mayor said as he heard a loud "Ain't that right!" coming from the back of the room where the former mayor and his group sat. "But if little Link Lake and rural communities like us are to continue, they must make some changes. Just look at all the changes we've already seen in our community, starting with several closed businesses. Change is hard; we all know that. But I firmly believe that there is an important difference between adjusting to changes raining down on us nearly every day and the changes we make with careful planning and strong support from our citizens. Do we want to be in charge of our changes, or are we willing to have others make them for us? Let's be in charge of the changes we need to make. What do you say?" There was a round of clapping, but not nearly as much as when Fred read his county fair memory.

"One of the challenges the Planning Commission is considering is helping our Link Lake community become energy independent. What does that mean? It means generating our own electricity and not being dependent on a big electric company to do it. How would we do it? One way is with solar panels; another is with wind turbines. Lot of folks don't much care for either of these ways to generate electricity, but they do work and work well. There's a third way the commission has been discussing. Most of you know Robert Spranger, who owns and operates the hardware store here in town. I've asked Robert to do some checking on the possibility of waterpower as a way of providing electricity to Link Lake."

Robert walked up to the podium and clicked on a computer projector. A picture of the Link Lake Mill, which had not been operating for many years, appeared on the screen.

"Everyone is familiar with the old mill, which the Village of Link Lake now owns. It stands empty—a building filled with memories. I've dug out a little history of this old mill.

"Jacob Johnson, an early settler in Link Lake, built the mill in 1873, the year after the village was established. He first constructed a dam on the Pine River, which flows through Link Lake. Rather than constructing a water wheel, which was common in those days when mills were constructed, he installed two penstocks in the dam. Each penstock allowed water to turn a turbine, which powered two millstones. One millstone ground wheat for flour, and the second ground oats and corn for cattle feed. Johnson's mill had to be one of the first ones to use a penstock with a turbine. James Francis, a British-American engineer, invented the first practical turbine in 1849.

"Arvin Johnson, Jacob's son, expanded the millpond, the dam, and the mill itself. With heavy rains, the dam often suffered damage as it had been constructed of rocks and soil. Arvin reinforced the dam with steel and concrete to make it more secure. In 1908, the dam's new generator began producing electricity for the Village of Link Lake, years ahead of when electricity came to the nearby farms.

"I've been doing some further checking, as I've heard about other communities that are relying on hydroelectric power."

"Thank you, Robert. An excellent report. Are there any questions?"

A hand went up from the second row. "Yes," the mayor said to the woman with a question.

"I heard when Link Lake previously had water-powered electricity that it was only turned on after dark and then turned off again at eleven at night. Is that true?"

"I've heard that, too," the mayor said, smiling. "I promise you, if we go the hydroelectric way, we'll have electricity twenty-four hours a day, seven days a week.

"So you all are aware of what our Planning Commission is doing. Besides doing some research on home-grown energy, we're discussing ways by which we can encourage our young high school graduates, many of whom go on to college, to come back to Link Lake to live and work. We're also looking at ways to encourage more retired people to live in Link Lake. We'll try to keep you all up-to-date as we continue our discussions. One answer is to make sure we have the best possible health care.

"During the COVID pandemic a few years ago, several young families moved here from Milwaukee and Madison and continued working. It became clear that we needed to upgrade our broadband internet system if working families would continue to move here and use computers to keep in touch with their supervisors and fellow workers. We also discovered that these mostly young families enjoyed our park, our lake, and our outdoor recreational activities.

The recently remodeled mercantile as a cultural arts center is a major step forward. We learned several of these families liked history—our museum needs some upgrading. We once had a village band—can we start another one? Our library is improving rapidly thanks to Jackie Jo, our head librarian, and the library board.

"These are some of the things our Planning Commission is discussing. We'll keep you informed. I'm pleased to see Andy Dee from WLLK-AM in the audience. Andy does a good job of keeping us all up-to-date on what's going on in Link Lake, besides providing a bit of a chuckle with the antics of Ole and Ollie."

15
Radio WLLK

"Good morning, everyone. This is Andy Dee coming to you from WLLK-AM, located here in downtown Link Lake, Wisconsin. The temperature at nine o'clock is sixty degrees. The sky is clear with a light breeze.

"I know you've been waiting to hear what's going on with Ole and Ollie. Here's what I recently learned.

Ole asked his friend, Ollie, when they met on the street the other day, 'What's new?'

"Ollie says, 'Not much, except I did see my old friend Linky Lathrop the other day. Haven't seen old Linky for many a moon. Hardly recognized the old bugger.'

"'So how'd that go? Learn anything new from Linky?' Ole asked.

"'I did learn something,' Ollie said. 'I asked old Linky how he was doing,'

"'What'd he tell ya?'

"'He said he was born with nothing, and he had most of it left.'

"More wisdom from Ole and Ollie tomorrow," Andy said, chuckling.

"Now on to the news, but first, the weather report. High today around seventy-five degrees with a cool ten-mile-per-hour breeze. Fifty degrees tomorrow morning with some showers coming. Could use a little rain. Corn crop needs it, and so do the potatoes.

"The big news in Link Lake these days is the work of the mayor's Planning Commission. I attended the recent community meeting where Mayor Jon Jessup shared some of the commission's present thinking. A second group helping out the Planning Commission is a writers' group taught by Jackie Jo Jensen, our library director. This group is focusing on the history of Link Lake. Jessup says we can't know where we're going until we know where we've been. With that in mind, farmer Fred Russo read a piece about his 4-H calf named Thunder. Everyone in the audience found it most interesting, me included. For the former 4-H members in the group, it brought back lots of memories.

"Today I'm pleased to have with me as a guest on WLLK, former mayor of Link Lake, Olaf Knudson. Good to have you with us, Olaf. It's been a while since you've been on *The Voice of Reason* show with me. Not since Jon Jessup won the last election."

"That's right," said Olaf. "But you know this Jessup guy really didn't win the election; I did. There was something crooked going on in the counting. I'm sure of it. I'm really still the mayor of Link Lake."

"Really," Andy Dee said. He, of course, had heard this before from Olaf and from several of his loyal followers. Changing the subject, Andy asked Olaf what he thought of Fred Russo's story about his 4-H calf at the fair.

"Story was okay, but it was stupid. What's taking a calf to the Ames County Fair got to do with helping Link Lake solve some of its problems? Not one thing. Not a single one. Nothing at all to do with what the mayor says it wants to do.

"This mayor is dumb as a stump. Brings up this environmental bunk. This climate change stuff. We all know it's just a hoax. Weather's been changing since the beginning of time. What in blue blazes does talking about the environment have anything to do with anything? It's just plain dumb. Heard them talking about having the old mill generate electricity for our village—just a stupid idea. Why do you suspect the village quit doing it—and they did—and hooked themselves up to the power grid way back in the 1930s? Dumbest idea that ever came down the road—looking back to waterpower for electricity.

"You know, don't you, that this Jessup guy was fired from his job in a community up north. Know why he was fired? Because he was pushing these dumb ideas that he's pushing here. He isn't even from around here. He's a city guy. What in blue blazes does a city guy know what's needed here in the country? Not a single thing does he know about us and what's important to us. Not a thing. He just doesn't belong here.

"Do you know what's going to happen? And your listeners are the first to hear it. I am passing around a petition to hold a recall election to get rid of this guy. He don't belong here, and the sooner we git rid of him, the better. The way he's going, he'll destroy Link Lake."

"We're out of time. But I'm sure we'll hear a lot more about this," said Andy Dee. "Thanks for coming on the air with me."

"The old Norwegian says, 'If you've got nothing to say, please don't say it.'"

16
Fred and Oscar

Oscar arrived at the café and sat down in his reserved chair just as Fred entered the restaurant. Before Fred could even sit down, Oscar said, "Did you listen to WLLK-AM this morning?"

"Nope, I didn't. I can't take those dumb Ole and Ollie stories on the morning program. They are just too dang dumb."

"You missed some big news. Really big news," Oscar said.

"What happened? Somebody's barn burn down?"

"No barn burned down. News worse than that," Oscar said.

"So you gonna tell me the news before my fresh cup of coffee Pauline just poured me gets cold?"

"Hold your horses, Fred. I'm just about to tell you."

"Well, about time," Fred said.

"We are having a recall election here in Link Lake," said Oscar quietly.

"A what?"

"A recall election," Oscar said a little louder.

"Who?"

"Olaf Knudson, the former mayor, has a petition going around for people to sign. He wants to get rid of Mayor Jessup," said Oscar.

"Why the hell does he want to do that? Old Olaf lost the election to Jessup fair and square," said Fred.

"That's not what Olaf thinks. He believes he was cheated in the last election and that he should still be mayor now. To hear Olaf talk, we now have the worst mayor ever, and the sooner we get rid of him, the better off we'll be," said Oscar. "I heard him. Couldn't believe what I was hearing."

"Geez," said Fred. "That old bastard is gonna tear our village in two. Lots of folks liked him when he was mayor, you know. He was intent on taking the village back to where it had been in the 1950s, but it didn't work."

"Our new mayor got me thinking for sure," Oscar said. "I hadn't thought much about the fact that maybe we can change things the way we want and not wait for change to come to us on its own. And I like his idea, too, of looking at where we have been and then taking the good things from that and building it into where we ought to be headed."

"Olaf called Mayor Jessup 'dumb as a stump.' He ought to look in the mirror. Olaf hasn't had a new idea in ten years," said Oscar. "Olaf is especially down on Jessup's ideas about dealing with climate change—says it's a big hoax and makes no sense at all. Olaf thinks Jessup's idea of the village making its own electricity is the dumbest idea to ever come down the road. I'd say let's give it a try."

"I'm with you on that," said Fred.

"By the way, Fred, for being a person who said he didn't know how to write, you did a heckuva job with the story about your bull calf at the county fair when you were twelve years old. Got me and a bunch of other people thinking about the time when we were 4-H members."

"Thank you," said Fred. "That Jackie Jo is quite the teacher. She's got a bunch of us thinking about stuff we haven't thought about for a long time. Been kind of fun."

17
Writing Class

When Jackie Jo walked from the Williams House to the library on Saturday morning, she noticed it was hot, cloudy, and very humid. She never paid much attention to the weather, but this morning, for some reason it seemed different. She couldn't quite figure out what was different about it. The weather in Link Lake was always a mystery to her as it was constantly changing—sometimes to her liking and sometimes not. It was time for the regular writing class to meet once more. Jackie Jo asked Ezra Brown, pastor of the Church of Peace in Link Lake, and Emily Higgins, from the Link Lake Historical Society, if they'd do some digging into the background and early history of the village. Most of the town's older folks knew that the village was named after a preacher from New York State who had come to Wisconsin. Pastor Brown and Emily agreed to share what they'd learned so far with the writing class.

Jackie Jo met Emily shortly after Jackie Jo took the job at the library. They discovered early on that they had similar interests, even though Emily was old enough to be Jackie Jo's grandmother.

When Jackie Jo first met Pastor Brown, she thought he was just another one of those stuffed shirt preachers she'd heard about. She'd come in contact with several and wanted nothing to do with any of them. It didn't help that when she first met Pastor Brown, he had asked her if she'd found Jesus. She'd thought it was none of his business whether she'd found Jesus or not.

But as the weeks sped by, and she had held several writing sessions, she had developed a new opinion of Pastor Brown. He had a keen sense of humor, he was a willing participant in class discussions, and he, at least according to Jackie Jo, didn't act like a pastor, especially not like those she had previously known.

Everyone appeared on time, enjoying the air-conditioned room on a hot and humid day. The topic of the day was the radio show that everyone in the class had heard and learned about the upcoming recall election of Mayor Jessup.

"Can't believe it's happening," said Fred Russo. "My old friend Oscar Anderson—he's on the mayor's Planning Commission—and I talked about this the other day. I think it's just a dumb thing for old former Mayor Knudson to do. I always kind of liked old Olaf, but it sounds like he's gone off the rails."

"Sounds that way," said Joe January. "Too bad. All this recall stuff can sure screw up our current mayor's plans for helping Link Lake work out its future."

"I must say, as I watched and listened to what the mayor is promoting, former Mayor Olaf Knudson may have it right," said Lucy Miller quietly. She was a member of the writing class but seldom said anything, and Jackie Jo wasn't aware that she was writing anything either.

"Maybe it's high time we cut the new mayor's cord and get back to the sensible stuff that my friend Olaf Knudson has been promoting for the past ten years. Like keeping taxes down and spending as little money as possible," said Lucy. "As I listen to you folks, I don't believe I belong in this group. You are sounding like a bunch of misguided liberals who want to try all kinds of dumb things with our country and with our wonderful little Link Lake. I like it just as we are." Lucy closed her notebook, got out of her chair, and headed for the library door, which she slammed behind her.

"Well, that's a surprise," said Jackie Jo. "I knew she had conservative leanings, but that was one of the reasons I was glad to have her in the class. I thought maybe she'd have some bank stories, being the wife of the former bank president. Stories beyond when the bank was robbed in 1940. I thought the group would benefit from having a variety of perspectives."

"I thought the purpose of this group was to write down some of the history of Link Lake, to be of help to the mayor's Planning Commission," said Carolyn with a rather surprised look on her face after Lucy abruptly left the group. "I'll talk to Lucy and see if I can convince her to rejoin us. I, for one, would like to hear some more bank stories. I wonder if she has a take on what happened to the stolen money."

"I'd like to know more about that, too," said Jackie Jo, smiling. "If there's one historical question that everyone in Link Lake seems to have on their mind, it's, 'What happened to the bank robbery money?'"

Jackie Jo took a deep breath. "Well, let's move on. I know Pastor Brown and Emily have been working on how Link Lake got its name and what it was like when the village first got started. Who's gonna start?"

"I'll begin," said Pastor Brown. "First the name. How did Link Lake get its name? Well, the village is named after a rather unusual pastor by the name of Increase Joseph Link. He named the village he started after himself, as well as the lake that everyone enjoys.

"Emily and I have been working closely with the Wayne County New York Historical Society, which has a separate room devoted to the history of Pastor Link, who had become quite famous. But let me start at the beginning: Increase Joseph Link grew up on a farm near the village of Plum Falls, New York. Young Increase Joseph wasn't interested in farming but thought preaching might be interesting. He enrolled in a New York seminary. This was in 1848. He was there for less than a semester when he was expelled. His seminary instructors did not appreciate his questioning of long-standing theological beliefs. One of his instructors had written that Increase Joseph would never make a decent preacher. Crestfallen, he returned to the home farm, helping his father with the everyday farm work, which he increasingly disliked.

"Two years later, in 1850, Increase Joseph married a local girl, Elwina Grabholtz, and they soon had a little boy. But then a catastrophe visited Increase Joseph, who continued working on the home farm. He went to fetch the cows from their night pasture one stormy summer morning. He was struck by lightning, and his family believed he had been killed. His normally dark hair had turned pure white. He had not been killed but was unable to talk for several days. As he began to talk once more, he constantly mumbled the words, 'Message, message.'

"Soon he was speaking single words and then sentences. Family and friends believed that the lightning strike had turned him a bit daft, as he spoke to cows, to the family dog, the hogs in the pigpen, a blue jay sitting in a tree above him. Why was he doing this? Because of the message he said he had received directly from God that he 'must rise up and speak.' And that's what he began doing. He was planning to go to Plum Falls and speak from the bandstand in the center of town, but he first had to be ready, as he preached to every living creature he could find.

"Emily and I have had a grand time digging out this history of Increase Joseph. She'll now continue with the story," said Pastor Brown.

18
Preacher Increase Joseph

"Thank you, Ezra," Emily began. "Before I continue, I want to say what a pleasure it has been working with Pastor Brown on this project. It seemed every day we worked on it, we discovered something new. Sometimes it was a bit strange, other times more than a bit strange. I also want to thank the Wayne County New York Historical Society for all their help. They have collected stories, letters, journal entries, and more about Increase Joseph Link, who began his career in little Plum City, Wayne County, New York. But now let me continue with the story of this man who became a famous pastor, if not a bit of a strange one.

"It was on a warm July Saturday in 1850 when Increase Joseph drove the family team and buggy to Plum City, where he tied up the team and stepped up onto the bandstand. He wore black pants, a black coat, and a black hat. According to a letter written by one of the bystanders on that day, Increase Joseph began with the words: 'Sisters and brothers, I stand before you on this beautiful evening to bring you a word from God.' Several people had gathered to hear what this guy with the white hair and dressed in black had to say. With a loud, clear voice, this strange speaker proceeded, 'We are destroying our land. How, you ask? We are destroying our land by allowing the waters from heaven to wash it away. We are destroying our land by allowing the winds to blow it away. We are destroying our land by allowing crops to grow where no crops should be grown. We have forgotten that we are from the land, and to the land we will return. It's the land that nourishes us and gives us life. We must learn to love the land as we love God.'

"As he spoke, his words became louder, and soon a larger crowd had gathered. Someone close to the bandstand noticed that Increase Joseph was holding a red book. Earlier, he had remembered that preachers always carried a bible. He believed he should carry some kind of book as well, so he found a dusty red book in the parlor of the home farm and brought it with him to Plum Falls. 'What's that red book yer carrin'?' the scruffy fellow asked. 'Why don't you read from it?'

"Increase Joseph opened the red book and read, 'The land comes first. It's the land. Unless we take care of it, we shall all perish.'

"The fellow asking the question laughed, 'You ain't no preacher. You sound like a crazy man—ain't you the guy who was struck by lightnin' a while back? Made you crazy.'

"Okay," Emily said. "I'll turn the story back to you, Ezra."

Ezra began reading. "By the late winter of 1852, Pastor Increase Joseph, as he was commonly known, had convinced a small group of farmers and small business people from Plum Falls that his weekly Saturday talk was more interesting than the sermons their traditional church pastors yelled out. It seems the traditional pastors had but two themes that they never drifted away from. 'You are all sinners, and forever will be, and give more money to the church so you can be saved from eternal damnation.'

"Pastor Increase Joseph learned that Wisconsin had become a state in 1848 and had recently signed a treaty with the Indian tribe that had been in central Wisconsin for many years to sell their lands to the U.S. government. These lands were now available for settlement. Pastor Increase Joseph, constantly mocked and belittled for his strange views and equally weird Saturday night talks, was ready to leave the area. He shared his idea for moving to Wisconsin, and about thirty of his most devoted followers agreed to go with him.

"In April 1952, the small group, now calling themselves the Standalone Fellowship, set out for Buffalo, New York, where Great Lakes ships were making regular trips to the west, including Wisconsin. Arriving in Sheboygan, the group headed west to central Wisconsin, where they hoped to find a place to settle. They spent a night at Wade House and then traveled on to Fond du Lac. After a few more miles, they arrived at the Fox River, where a makeshift ferry took them and their belongings across. Traveling a bit farther, they came upon a beautiful, blue water lake with no settlement of any kind on it. Pastor Increase Joseph was quite taken with what he saw. By the way, how do we know all this? It seems several people in the Standalone Fellowship wrote letters to their relatives back in Plum Falls. The Wayne County Historical Society has a collection of what they call the Increase Joseph Link Letters.

"Stopping his wagon and team at the water's edge, Increase Joseph, with his ever-present red book in hand, jumped down and began wading into the lake fully clothed. His followers watched, wondering what their rather eccentric leader was up to now. When the water was up to his waist, he lifted the red book high over his head. There was no sound. Even the spring birds that were singing ceased their songs. In a loud voice, Increase Joseph began speaking. 'God has brought us to this new place, and for that we are eternally grateful.' He began waving the red book back and forth over his head. 'This body of water shall forever, from this day forward, be known as Link Lake. And this settlement,' he waved his red book toward the open land around Link Lake, 'will also be forever known as Link Lake, Wisconsin.'

"His travel-tired followers all began clapping, as they now knew what to call this place located in the wilds of Wisconsin that had been Indian land for thousands of years. They immediately began building log cabins, barns, and even a couple of buildings for the small businessmen in the group. A log church was the last building completed. It was a challenge to build because Increase Joseph insisted it be round. 'There is no place to hide in a round church,' intoned Pastor Increase Joseph. It is about impossible to build a round log building. The Standalone Church had sixteen sides. Pastor

Increase Joseph found a place for the church, a small hill not far from his cabin, a place that commanded a view of the lake and all of its beauty.

"Church services were held every Sunday afternoon for the Standalone Fellowship as it slowly grew when more settlers moved into and around Link Lake. One of the church members believed the church should have its own hymn, one that would show the uniqueness of the Standalone Fellowship. She titled the hymn 'We Are Alone Together':

> *We are alone together,*
> *Of God and the land.*
> *Yet together we stand*
> *As alone we are, too,*
> *Simple yet not,*
> *A direction but no.*
> *We stand for the land,*
> *May it ever be so.*

"That's how Link Lake got its name. Many of us were probably unaware that Increase Joseph and his Standalone Church could be called our first environmentalists. Increase Joseph went on to preach the virtues of caring for the land near and far, drawing huge audiences, many just to hear this man with a loud, clear voice and an entertaining way of speaking."

The writing group was clapping when Ethyl Williams burst into the room, red-faced and excited. "There's a flood warning," she said. "Just heard it on the radio. We are expecting twelve inches of rain in the next few hours. It's pouring down rain right now," she said. "The warning said that anyone living close to Link Lake should evacuate to higher ground. Everyone in the Village of Link Lake can expect their basement to flood and, for many, the first floor of their homes."

Everyone got up, pulled on their jackets, and rushed to the door. They were greeted with heavy rain, coming down so hard they could barely see across the street from the library.

19

Flood

"What should we do?" said Ethyl, who was quite upset with the news. "The lake is not far from us—you think we'll be flooded?"

Jackie Jo looked out the window at the deluge of rain falling. Cars driving by on the street appeared to have water up to their car doors.

"We'd better get busy and take the books from the bottom shelves and pile them on top of the bookshelves," Jackie Jo said.

"But the library's never been flooded before. You think we need to do that?" Ethyl said.

"There's always a first time. I've been reading about entire towns flooding with the heavy rains falling in various parts of the country. It's this climate change that everyone is talking about. I think we'd better be safe than sorry and move the books on the lower shelves to a higher place. Hate to lose a bunch of books to a flood," Jackie Jo said.

Jackie Jo and Ethyl began moving books to higher surfaces in the library as the waters of Link Lake continued to rise. A police vehicle, higher off the ground than most vehicles, moved slowly down the street in front of the library. "Please evacuate immediately," shouted the voice from the police vehicle. "The Link Lake dam may break any minute and completely flood the village. Leave immediately."

Just then, Jackie Jo's cell phone rang. "This is Emily," a stressed voice loudly said. "Our basement is flooding. Send Ethyl home. I need help."

Jackie Jo passed the message on to Ethyl, and she grabbed her jacket and promptly left, leaving Jackie Jo to contend with the floodwaters that had nearly reached the library's front door. She could see the Link Lake dam out the library window, only a few blocks away, and if the floodwaters burst through it, the library would be destroyed. The concrete dam seemed to be holding; at least it looked that way to Jackie Jo.

The radio was playing polka music in the background. So far the library had power, but how long would that last? The "Beer Barrel Polka" was playing when it was abruptly interrupted. "This is the National Weather Service. Flood warning, flood warning. Evacuate low areas immediately. Heavy rain continues, and local dams are likely to break and cause severe flooding. Evacuate immediately."

Jackie Jo finished moving books on the library's first floor to higher shelves and prepared to leave and hurry back to the Williams House and her apartment. Maybe she could be of some help to Emily and Ethyl with their flooded basement. But then she thought about the library's basement, where the cleaning supplies, spare shelving, those sorts of things were stored. She had only been down there a few times since working at the library. She opened the door to the basement stairs and flipped on the light. She was aghast at what she saw. The basement was flooded. She saw water pouring in through the only window in the basement, which had shattered.

She pulled off her shoes and socks and rolled up her slacks. She grabbed hold of the stairway railing and was soon in water up to her knees. The water at the bottom of the stairs was well above her knees. She looked around at the flooded space with floating boxes of various sizes with cleaning supplies, she surmised. But then she saw what looked like a relatively large heavy cloth bag, different from the boxes of cleaning supplies. It was covered with mud that had seeped into the basement with the floodwater. But what was it, and what was in it? She waded over to where the big bag was floating, grabbed hold of it, and carried it back toward the stairway. It wasn't as heavy as she thought it might be, and she wondered where it came from and what was in it. She decided to carry it upstairs to find out. Once upstairs, she carried the dripping, muddy bag to the little kitchen at one end of the community room.

She found a brush and began scrubbing the mud off the bottom of the mysterious bag, which appeared to be waterproof. She scrubbed the dirty brown mud off the sides of the bag and then began working it off the top, which was zipped shut with what appeared to be a waterproof, heavy-duty zipper. The bag also had two cloth carrying handles. She worked around the handles and across the zipper to remove a couple layers of mud. Slowly, some words began to appear as she scrubbed.

20

Emergency

Mayor Jon Jessup called a special meeting of the Link Lake citizens, using local radio station WLLK to get the word out. Except for the basement, the library had been spared from the flood, so the community room was available for meetings. The power, which had been off for twenty-four hours, was also restored. The flood damage from some fifteen inches of heavy rain had ceased, and the Link Lake dam had thankfully remained intact.

About fifty of the Link Lake citizens who had answered the call to evacuate had spent the night at the Link Lake High School, where the Red Cross had come to provide meals and portable bunks. Most of the citizens had returned to their homes, many facing considerable flood damage, especially those with homes near the lake, which had run over its banks.

"Good afternoon," Mayor Jessup began, "and a good afternoon it is. Many of you have damage from the flood, but it could have been so much worse. I contacted FEMA, and their representative is already here. He is in the back of the room, ready to talk with any of you with severe damage and needing FEMA's assistance. At this point, does anyone have any questions?"

An older bearded fellow sitting toward the back of the room raised his hand. "Yes," said Mayor Jessup, recognizing Bill Augustine, one of former Mayor Olaf Knudson's strong supporters.

"Why did this happen? I thought all you guys in control of things would never let something like this happen. Who ever heard of people having flooding homes today? That was something that happened a hundred years ago," an angry Bill Augustine said loudly.

"I believe the answer is climate change."

"Climate change. Hell, we all know that's one of them Democrat Party hoaxes. I think it's the weather bureau's fault. They're supposed to be in charge of the weather these days, and they screwed up. They let this happen, and what are we gonna do about it?" Augustine was now nearly yelling as several of his neighbors looked over at him, some shaking their heads.

"I'm sorry, Bill," the mayor said. "The weather bureau is not in charge of what kind of weather we have, never have been, never will be. They've got all they can do to predict and report on the weather."

"So who is in charge of the weather, then?" Bill shouted. "Who in hell is in charge?"

A woman in the front row stood up and said in a loud, clear voice, "It's Mother Nature who is in charge of the weather." Several people in the audience laughed.

"So how do I get in touch with this Mother Nature person?" Bill yelled sarcastically.

"I'd like to continue with the meeting," Mayor Jessup said, now frustrated with what was happening.

"I know some of you are interested in what the Link Lake Planning Commission has been doing. We are making progress, but because of the flood we will not be meeting for a month to allow people to make the necessary repairs and cleanup from the flood.

"Anyone else have a question?" Mayor Jon had noticed that his nemesis, Bill Augustine, had left the meeting.

Jackie Jo sat in the back of the room, wondering if this was the time or place to share her news. It was but a few days ago, when she was dealing with a flooded library basement, that she found a mysterious canvas bag covered with mud from the flood. She remembered as she scrubbed off the mud that the words "Property of . . ." appeared.

A VILLAGE LOOKS AHEAD

The next words that came into view were "Link Lake." As the muddy water trickled away in the little kitchen's sink, one last word appeared: "Bank." With her arms covered with muddy water up to her elbows, it hit her. Could this be the missing money from the 1940 bank robbery? She carefully zipped open the bag and peered inside. It was stuffed full of money.

She dried her hands on a towel, walked to the front door, and locked it. This was not the time to have someone walk into the library, even in the midst of a flood cleanup, and see the librarian up to her elbows in money. She took the money-filled bag to her office and carefully began separating the bills according to their value, ranging from one-dollar bills up to hundred-dollar bills. She counted the money once she finished stacking the bills into their respective piles. It totaled $50,000. Jackie Jo had never seen so much money. What to do with it? For the time being, she decided to lock the money and the empty bag in the safe she had in her office.

Jackie Jo knew she had solved the decades-old mystery. But what should she do now? Who should she tell? Maybe tell nobody? Keep the answer to herself? The community had been discussing what happened that fateful day in 1940 for all of these years. People liked mysteries, she realized, especially when they were local and involved people they knew. Maybe she should keep it a mystery, keep people thinking about who had the money from the bank robbery. She needed some time to think about what to do. She thought of simply returning the money to the Link Lake Bank—it was their money, after all. Maybe she should turn it in at the police station. They would know what to do with it. For the time being, she would do nothing. It was in a place where no one could get at it. Only she had the code for the safe in her office. She wished she had someone to talk to about this. She wondered if the old saying "Finders keepers" was true. If so, we had, latterly, a pile of money in the library's safe.

21

Fred and Oscar

The two old farmers arrived at the Black Oak Café at the same time, one holding the door for the other. The café was built on higher ground, so it hadn't suffered flood damage. It also had a brisk business, as some people in town with flooded homes were eating there.

"So you get wet feet from the storm?" Oscar asked Fred as they removed their caps.

"Not me. How about you?" answered Fred.

"I remember what my pa said, and he said it often. 'Make sure when you build a house, to make sure it is on high ground, so you never have any problem with high water,'" Oscar said.

"Well, he sure had that right. Wonder how many folks flooded out. I saw one of the houses built near Link Lake tip over right into the lake. Sure hope the people got out first," said Fred.

"I've been helping out over at the high school. Some of the folks who had to leave their homes have been staying there. I've been helping the Red Cross and the National Guard, making meals and finding places for folks to sleep," said Oscar.

"Mighty good of you, Oscar. Bunch of folks lost everything. FEMA folks here to help them out," said Fred. "I've been busy, too, just so you know."

"Doing what?" asked Oscar.

"Helping old Bill Augustine clean up his place."

"You what?" said Oscar, with a surprised tone.

"I helped Bill Augustine clean up his house. Basement was full of water, and he even had some damage on the first floor. He's working on cleaning up the place all by himself," said Fred.

"Kind of made a fool out of himself at the community meeting," said Oscar.

"Old Bill's hurting, hurting bad. His wife died six months ago. She was a good friend of my wife," said Fred.

"I didn't know that," Oscar said. "Good for you, Fred."

"I remember my pa saying that just because you may not like your neighbor doesn't mean you don't help him out when he needs it. And old Bill really needed help, lots of it. We've got it cleaned up enough so at least he doesn't have to wade through water to get to the stairway and his upstairs bedroom that stayed dry," said Fred.

"It's gonna take a while, but it's good to see Link Lake people helping each other, even though they may not agree at times. Sometimes it takes a calamity like a flood to bring people together. Too bad about the flood, but it sure has brought people together. I haven't heard anybody talking about the recall election. Before the flood a bunch of people were anxious to get rid of our mayor. Not a word. I'm sure some of them were working elbow to elbow with the mayor over at the high school, helping him serve meals to the people with near ruined houses," said Oscar.

The two old friends continued eating breakfast, occasionally glancing out the window at the sunny day with a clear blue sky.

After a few minutes of quiet, Oscar asked, "So what's on your schedule today, Fred?"

"I told Bill I would stop by this morning to see if he needed any more help."

"I'm wondering how the library came out of all of this. I heard it had some water in the basement but nothing on the first floor," said Oscar. "That writing class of yours still meeting?"

"Jackie Jo said we'd take a break for a couple weeks, give people a chance to recover from the flood."

"Same with the mayor's Planning Commission. We're not meeting for another month," said Oscar.

22
Radio WLLK

"Good morning, everyone. This is Andy Dee with *The Voice of Reason*, coming to you from WLLK-AM in downtown Link Lake. The downtown, including the radio station, has mostly dried out from our recent historic flood. Seems this was the worst flood to ever come to Link Lake, and we all hope it's the last. One of those hundred-year events.

"Let's get started with Ole and Ollie. It seems Ole saw a sign in front of Ollie's lake cottage that said, 'Boat for Sale' propped against a rototiller and a lawn mower. Ole asked about the boat. 'Yup,' said Ollie. 'They are boat for sale.'

"What can I say that likely hasn't already been said about the flood? We've known for a long time that the people of Link Lake are good people. They know how to help each other when help is needed. Some of us had come to believe the village was coming apart at the seams—those who agreed with our mayor and his plans for making changes in the village, and those who didn't like him one bit and were setting out to recall him in an upcoming recall election.

"But then the rain began to fall and didn't quit until some fifteen inches fell on the lake and everywhere else, and the water ran over its banks and began rushing into town, not trickling but rushing. It took cars along with it, flooding them, tipping them over, and then tumbling them down Main Street one after the other, until leaving them ruined on people's flooded lawns. Not a pleasant thing to see. And not to forget about the dozens of flooded basements, some homes with flooded first floors, and one home caught in a mudslide that pushed it right into Link Lake, just its roof sticking out of the water.

"I'm privileged to have with me this morning Mayor Jon Jessup. I know he must be very busy these days. Good morning, Mayor. How are you?"

"I'm surviving," said the mayor. "My wife and I have been living at the high school, helping care for people who have flooded homes."

"I know people may be curious. How did your home make it through the flood?"

"Our house is on a little rise, and we had no damage. But our front yard is mostly gone. Some of the floodwaters rushed by the front of our house, taking our front yard, the sidewalk, and the drive to our garage with it. We have to park our car down the street from our house," said the mayor. "But our problems are nothing compared to some of my neighbors.

"The damage in our village is horrific, no question about it. But we will survive. As bad as it is, it doesn't compare with the flood damage in Florida or Western North Carolina. I want to thank the citizens of Link Lake, who have come together in a wonderful way to help each other. I know people have differences with each other these days, especially political differences, but they left all of that behind and rushed out to help each other. I am impressed and can't thank you all enough. Link Lake will survive this historic flood, and I predict it will be stronger than ever."

"Thank you, Mayor Jessup, for your support and your leadership," said Andy.

"To close this segment of our show, the old Norwegian says: 'Do the best you can with what you've got.'"

23

Ben Neverson

Benjamin Neverson, everyone called him Ben, had recently completed a graduate teaching degree in environmental studies at the University of Illinois. His master's degree research thesis focused on climate change. He had been an elementary teacher for a few years. At age twenty-five, his interests had changed to researching and teaching about climate change. He was tall, with blond hair and blue eyes, and kept himself in good physical shape by hiking, swimming, and playing basketball in pick-up games. He had been in a relationship with another graduate student, but as the months passed, that relationship cooled and then fizzled out. He was now looking for a high school teaching job and noticed the listing for a high school science teacher that Link Lake High School had recently posted. He applied.

Ben was born and raised in Chicago but didn't like big cities and looked forward to working in a smaller town. Link Lake seemed to be just what he was looking for. His interview with the high school principal, Jane Watson, went well. He learned that the village had recently flooded, and the cleanup was mostly completed, with neighbors helping neighbors with the work. When he learned about the flood, including the lake running over its banks and some mudslides that caused considerable damage, he immediately thought of his research on climate change. What happened here was an excellent example of what was often a result of a changing climate. He thought he could probably use Link Lake's flood as a case study for his high school science classwork.

Principal Watson told him about the mayor's Planning Commission, which was looking toward the future of Link Lake, with a special focus on a future that was kind to the environment. He felt that the principal supported the mayor's efforts. The principal didn't share that the mayor was facing a recall election because a substantial number of citizens liked the old Link Lake and were turned off by what the mayor had been suggesting. Principal Watson told Ben about the Link Lake Library, which had an active writing class focusing on the village's history. "The writing class was also the mayor's suggestion. One of the mayor's favorite sayings is, 'We can't know where we are going until we know where we have been.' Our librarian, Jackie Jo Jensen, is teaching the writing class and is doing an excellent job."

At the end of the interview, when Ben learned he had been hired, Principal Watson asked him if he had a preference for where he would like to live. Not knowing if he would land the job, Ben had not thought much about where he'd like to live other than believing he should live right here in Link Lake and not in one of the nearby cities where the principal had said some of the teachers lived.

"The Williams House has apartments for rent. It's an old railroad hotel, but when the railroad pulled up its rails and left town, it became an apartment building. You'll find the Williams sisters interesting, with lots of stories to tell about the early days in Link Lake."

"Thank you," Ben said, standing and shaking the principal's hand. I'm looking forward to teaching here, and I will stop by the Williams House to see if there are any apartments for rent."

Principal Watson pointed in the direction of the Williams House. Ben drove his well-worn Honda Accord the few blocks to the house and parked on the street. He looked up at this three-story, well-kept house and wondered what it was like inside and what it would be like living here. It appeared to be located in a quiet part of Link Lake. Ben soon learned that all of Link Lake was quiet.

He walked up to the front door along a walkway lined with rose bushes. Two rocking chairs sat on the big porch surrounding the big old house. He rang the doorbell, and after a short wait, the door opened.

"How can I help you?" said an older, gray-haired woman with one hand on the door.

"My name is Ben Neverson, and I've just been hired as the new science teacher at the high school. The principal said you might have a spare apartment for rent."

"Come in, come in. I'm Emily Williams. My twin sister, Ethyl, and I own this place."

"Thank you," Ben said. He walked into a living room that appeared decorated like something he might see in the 1950s, but he didn't say anything.

"Yes, we have a one-bedroom apartment for rent right here on the ground floor. Follow me. I'll show it to you."

Ben looked around. Everything appeared spotlessly clean, even though it was old.

"Here it is," Emily said, opening a door with 101 on it.

Emily proceeded to show Ben the apartment. It had a small living room with a window that looked out on the street, a tiny kitchen, one nice-sized bedroom, and a bathroom. "Not all of our apartments have their own bathroom, but this one does. What do you think?" Emily asked.

"Looks good to me! How much a month?" Emily mentioned a number.

"That's fine," Ben said. He was thinking how much less a month this one was compared to a similar-sized apartment in Chicago.

"Oh, by the way. Your neighbor on the second floor is Jackie Jo Jensen. She is very busy as Link Lake's librarian, but she's home nearly every evening."

"Yes, Principal Watson mentioned her. Said she was teaching a writing class about the early history of Link Lake."

"Yup, she is, and the writing class is coming up with some interesting events, history that I never heard about."

Ben remembered that he hadn't eaten since breakfast and asked if there were any good places to eat in Link Lake.

"Only one place," said Emily, "but it's good. That's what I hear from folks who've eaten there anyway. It's right on Main Street, called the Black Oak Café."

"Thank you," Ben said. He headed to his Honda and drove toward downtown Link Lake. On the way, he passed a well-maintained building with a flower bed alongside its front door. Above the door was a sign that read, "Increase Joseph Memorial Library."

I should stop here after I eat, thought Ben. *See what books they have related to climate change and meet my new neighbor.* Within a few minutes, he was driving down Main Street and spotted the Black Oak Café just ahead. He parked in front and went inside. He was immediately engulfed by the smells of fresh coffee brewing and something cooking in the kitchen.

"Can I show you to a table?" an older-looking, smiling waitress asked.

"Sure," said Ben. He was again impressed with another friendly Link Lake person.

"How about a cup of freshly made coffee?" she asked. "My name is Pauline, and the special today is beef stew," she said, "with homemade bread."

"Coffee and beef stew it is," said Ben, smiling. He glanced around the restaurant and spotted about half a dozen other customers. Occasionally, someone would look in his direction.

His coffee, stew, and bread soon arrived, and he began eating. He couldn't remember when he tasted better stew. And homemade bread. He hadn't eaten homemade bread since he was a kid when his mother occasionally baked bread.

After eating, Ben drove down Main Street, spotting Spranger Hardware, the Link Lake Mercantile, and nearby Link Lake Bank. He saw a big white church on a little hill at the end of Main Street. Near the front door was a sign: "Church of Peace: Everyone Welcome. Ezra Brown, Pastor." None of these buildings seemed harmed by the recent flood Principal Watson had talked about. He was about to drive to the library when his cell phone rang. *Who could be calling*, he wondered.

"This is Ben," he said as he parked his car in the street across from the bank.

"Ben Neverson," a friendly voice said. "I'm Mayor Jon Jessup. I just got a call from Principal Jane Watson over at the high school. She said you've just been hired as the high school's new science teacher."

"That's right," Ben said, wondering why in the world he was getting a call from the village's mayor. He wouldn't begin teaching until the following week.

24
Chat with the Mayor

"First, congratulations on your new job. Link Lake may not be very big, but we've got a good high school. I think you'll like the school as well as living here. I assume you found a place to rent at the Williams House?" asked Mayor Jessup.

Ben thought, *Word sure moves fast here in Link Lake. Principal Watson must have told the mayor she had suggested the Williams House as a place to live.*

"Yes, I did," Ben answered. "Seems like a comfortable place, and the price is right." Ben couldn't imagine the mayor would call every new teacher who came to town.

"Have you got any extra time this afternoon?" the mayor asked.

"Well, yes, I do," Ben said. All he had to do was prepare a bit for the orientation meeting planned for the next day and prepare some lesson plans for next week. Nothing more. He thought he might visit Link Lake Park on the lake and sit and look at the water. He hadn't done that in a long while and was looking forward to it. But the mayor had something else in mind.

"Would you have a few minutes to stop by my office this afternoon?" asked the mayor.

"Sure," Ben said, wondering what possible reason the mayor had for talking with a new high school science teacher who hadn't even started teaching yet. "I could be there in a few minutes."

The mayor explained where the city hall was located—on one end of Main Street. Ben had spotted it earlier. He drove around the block, his mind filled with questions: *What if the mayor doesn't like me and gets me fired before I even begin teaching? With a master's degree, why had I applied for a teaching job in their little village?* But then Ben thought, *He did congratulate me on getting the job here. Why would he do that if he had something else on his mind?*

Ben parked in front of the city hall, walked up several steps, and pulled the heavy door open. Once inside, he saw a sign: "Mayor's Office, Room 101." He walked by an office with a temporary sign: "Federal Emergency Management Agency." FEMA. He then remembered that Link Lake recently had serious flood damage when the lake ran over its banks, and the dam nearly burst.

Ben stopped at the mayor's door and saw a smaller sign that read, "Come in." He opened the door and saw a middle-aged woman with graying hair working at a computer. Turning away from the computer, the woman with a professional but friendly voice asked, "What can I do for you?"

"I'm Ben Neverson. The mayor called me and said he wanted to talk with me."

"Yes, Ben. Welcome to Link Lake, and congratulations. I understand you are going to be our new science teacher over at the high school. I'm Gladys Westerly, and my husband, Floyd, is the janitor at the high school. You'll meet him once you start work over there. The mayor is waiting to talk with you. I'll tell him you are here." She got up and quietly knocked on the door behind her desk. "Ben Neverson is here."

"Send him in," Ben heard the mayor say. Ben took a big breath and walked into the mayor's office.

"Good afternoon, Mr. Neverson," said Mayor Jessup, who got up, walked around his desk, and extended his hand to Ben. "Thanks for stopping by."

"Glad to do it," said Ben. "Just call me Ben. Everyone does."

"Okay, have a chair, Ben." The mayor pointed to a little table in his office with two chairs next to it. "How has Link Lake been treating you?"

"I haven't been here a day yet, but I am impressed with how friendly everyone is."

"Principal told me you grew up in Chicago," said the mayor.

"I did," said Ben, wondering where this conversation was going and why he was sitting in the mayor's office only a few hours after being hired.

"Principal told me you just finished doing a master's degree at the University of Illinois. That's a good school."

"I have no complaints," said Ben. "It was a lot of work, especially in my area of interest."

"Principal Watson said your interest was researching climate change, right?"

"Yup. I've been interested in climate change since high school," said Ben. "Gotta get more people interested, especially in what to do about it."

"I couldn't agree with you more," said the mayor.

Ben was surprised to hear what the mayor said. He knew that almost half of the population, especially in some rural areas, thought climate change was a hoax. Many of these folks said that the climate is always changing.

The mayor jumped in. "Problem is what can we do about slowing climate change down without spending all of our resources putting things back together after one of the climate change storms comes our way."

"Agreed," said Ben quietly. He wondered how much of what he believed and knew about climate change he should share on his first day in rural Link Lake.

"I'm sure you've seen some of what a recent rainstorm did to our village and the farms around it," said the mayor. "The lake literally ran over, filling the basements of homes and sometimes much more. Thankfully, the community came together, and we are nearly back to where we were before this huge storm that flooded our little village."

"I see that," said Ben.

"Well, to get down to why I wanted to chat with you. You probably haven't heard that some months ago I appointed a Planning Commission made up of locals to look at Link Lake's future and explore the steps it ought to take to get there. One of the topics we wanted to explore was what we should do about climate change in our long-range planning for the village. Ironically, the flood caused by climate change put everything on hold. We haven't met for several weeks, but we'll meet again soon."

Ben listened carefully and agreed with nearly everything the mayor said but wondered, *Why is he telling me all this? I am merely a high school science teacher who will be discussing climate change in my classroom—period.*

The mayor stopped talking for a minute and looked out his office window at the activities on Main Street. Most of it was normal stuff, but some was still repair work left over from the flood.

"You don't have to answer me now," the mayor began, looking at Ben. "Would you consider being a member of our Planning Commission? We need someone with your research knowledge of climate change. It would surely help our discussions. I think you would be a great addition to our group, and besides, you might get some ideas to add to your research interest."

The mayor's request came as a complete surprise to Ben. He'd just been hired as a high school science teacher, and now, after meeting with the mayor for half an hour, he is invited to be a member of the mayor's Planning Commission.

"I-I don't know what to say," said Ben.

"Don't say anything. Take your time, think about it, and let me know your decision in a couple of days." The mayor got up, shook Ben's hand, and returned to his chair behind his desk.

Ben returned to his Honda, thinking about the conversation he'd just had with the mayor. He was more than a little overwhelmed that the mayor had asked him to be a member of an important Planning Commission.

25

Ben Meets Jackie Jo

His mind a scramble of thoughts, Ben drove to Link Lake Park, turned off his car, and sat looking at the lake, now nearly smooth as no wind was blowing, but still high and over its banks in many places. Ben was thinking about all that had happened in his life in the last few months.

He thought about Cindy Overstreet, with whom he had lived while in graduate school at the University of Illinois. She was also working on a graduate degree in anthropology and finished her master's degree the same time Ben did. She looked forward to working for a museum in one of the country's larger cities, preferably in Washington, D.C., or in New York. Ben was interested in teaching science in a small rural town, where he could focus on his interest in environmental concerns, especially climate change. His big question these days was: How is climate change affecting rural America?

He and Cindy parted quietly, each well aware of their fundamental preference as to where they wanted to live. One day they were living together, and the next day they were not—each going their separate ways. Those were sad days for Ben. He thought he was in love with Cindy and that she was in love with him. He was planning on getting married when both he and Cindy had jobs. But then he discovered she really was more interested in where she wanted to live than in

Ben. Hardly a day went by that his thoughts didn't return to Cindy and the good times they had together in graduate school. She was a good listener. Ben remembered sharing with her everything from questions about a graduate course he was taking to why it was important to stay away from too much booze. He saw what happened to some of his friends who proceeded to get drunk if they faced a problem. Ben had talked with Cindy when he faced hurdles he had trouble getting past. She was a huge help to him when he faced troubled times. But now he was alone. No Cindy. No friends nearby and now living in a small rural community after spending all of his life in cities many times larger than Link Lake, Wisconsin.

He thought about his meeting with the mayor. As he thought about it, this seemed most unusual. How many new high school teachers have a meeting with the local mayor, even before they begin teaching? He was betting the percentage would be zero. Mayor Jon Jessup was a long way from what he thought a small rural village mayor would be like. The mayor was thinking about the village's future and was aware of how climate change might have a major influence on Link Lake's future. Ben would let the mayor know he would be honored to be a part of the mayor's Planning Commission.

Returning to his car, Ben checked his watch. There was still time to stop at the library. He wanted to check what books they may have related to environmental concerns, especially climate change. One thing he noticed after his brief time in Link Lake—it didn't take long to get from one place to another. Within less than five minutes, he was parked in front of the Link Lake Memorial Library. He had about an hour before closing time.

Once inside, Ben stopped and looked around. He couldn't remember ever being in such a small library and immediately wondered if they would have anything of interest. About halfway along one wall of the library, he spotted a desk with a young woman seated behind it. Could this be Jackie Jo Jensen, the head librarian? It couldn't be. His idea of a librarian was a woman with her hair up in a bun, glasses hanging on the end of her nose, a high, squeaky voice, and dressed like someone on their way to church. He walked over to the desk and stopped. A little sign at the front of the desk read, "Director."

"Something I can help you with?" Jackie Jo asked.

Ben thought, *This library director does not meet any of my stereotypes of a librarian. This is one good-looking young woman.*

"You wouldn't be Jackie Jo Jensen?" Ben asked.

"That's me." Jackie Jo stood up from behind her desk. "And you are?"

"Benjamin Neverson, but everybody calls me Ben. I'm the new high school science teacher."

"Welcome to Link Lake. Where are you from?"

"Chicago, but most recently from Champaign-Urbana, where I was in graduate school."

"Well, Link Lake is not like either of those places, but I think you'll like it here. Very friendly people. I'm sure you are well aware the community is just getting past suffering from a flood that filled up a bunch of basements and even destroyed a few homes."

"I am," said Ben. "I also learned that the flood brought the community together—everyone helping everyone else."

"Yes, it did. It was really something to see," said Jackie Jo.

"Library damaged?"

"A little. We had water in our basement, but it didn't get to the first floor." Her mind immediately flashed to the waterproof bank pouch she found, filled with stolen bank money from the 1940 robbery. "You've probably noticed that there are no books on the lower shelves. We moved everything to higher places. Turned out we didn't need to, but you know the old saying, 'Better to be safe than sorry.' It's none of my business, but have you found a place to stay?" Jackie Jo was fast discovering how easy it was to talk with Ben. He looked at her with the bluest eyes she had ever seen. They seemed to sparkle when he talked. She began to have a feeling she hadn't had in a long time as she continued talking to this very attractive high school science teacher.

"Yes, I've found a place to stay. It's at the Williams House. I have a small apartment there."

"Guess what?" said Jackie Jo, smiling. "I have an apartment at the

Williams House as well."

"So we are neighbors," said Ben, remembering that Emily Williams told him Jackie Jo would be his neighbor. He was thinking, *This is a young woman I'd like to get to know better.*

"Almost forgot. One of the reasons I stopped in this afternoon was to see if you had any books on climate change," said Ben.

"Follow me." Jackie Jo came from behind her desk and walked to a bookshelf toward the back of the library. She pointed at two rows of books with various titles related to climate change.

"Wow," said Ben. "The big libraries I've been to in Chicago don't have as many climate change books as you do."

"Thanks to Mayor Jon Jessup, he gave us some extra money from the village's budget to buy climate change books," said Jackie Jo.

26

Radio WLLK

"Good morning, everyone. This is your morning radio host, Andy Dee, bringing you *The Voice of Reason* from downtown Link Lake, Wisconsin. It is a sunny, clear day, and according to the weather people, it will be like that all day.

"Before we get started with a very busy morning in radio land, I want to add my thanks to the many people in our village who stepped up to help during the recent flood, which I must say caught all of us by surprise. So many of you had flooded basements. And many of you had water rushing in the front door of your home and ruining everything on the first floor. Although you might not agree that anything good was left from that miserable flood, it did bring our community together. Friend and foe worked shoulder to shoulder to help those who suffered unbelievable losses from the wild water.

"Wondering what Ole and Ollie were doing? Well, they were mostly chatting with each other about the past. It was Ole who said to Ollie, 'Some of the best of what is next has been here all along.' I don't know if he was talking about people helping other people, but he could have, as our little community has a long history of helping each other when difficult times arise.

"I had the opportunity to sit in on a meeting of the mayor's Planning Commission. This was their first meeting since the flood.

Most of their discussion was about how to prevent future floods. Henry Swenson, the village maintenance man, pointed out that the dam at the end of the lake needed a complete overhaul.

"'It came as a whisper of busting open,' Henry said. 'Next big rain storm and the dam's likely to break, and then all hell will happen. If we think we have flooding problems with this last storm, that's nothing compared to what we can expect if the dam goes out. We've got to get right at fixing the dam, and then I'd recommend we build up the shore around the lake adjacent to the village. Build a kind of levee.'

"The mayor interrupted Henry. 'I agree completely with Henry's assessment. The village council has already discussed and approved both the repair of the dam as well as working on building a levee along the lake. I've contacted several contractors who do this type of work. We've already selected one and are starting work here in a week or two,' the mayor said.

"As you may recall," Andy Dee said, "the mayor's commission had been discussing how the village and the farms surrounding it might develop their own energy source and be off the grid, so to speak. They had been talking about renovating the dam and the generator that had been installed back in the early 1900s to generate electricity for the village. With the flood, that idea is off the table. We are lucky the dam is still in place, but the flood appears to have ruined any plans for generating electricity with waterpower. The members of the commission agreed that they should not go down that road, that the flood proved that waterpower generation would be too risky. So what next?

"The commission seemed stuck in their thinking. But a surprising thing happened. Link Lake High School's new science teacher, Ben Neverson, has a master's degree in environmental studies with a special focus on climate change. Principal Watson contacted the mayor about their new hire, and believe it or not, Ben is now a member of the Planning Commission.

"Ben shared some of his research knowledge with the Planning Commission. Most of the group was only vaguely familiar with what

Ben called geothermal energy. In language we all could understand, Ben began describing this energy source, which he simply said is heat energy from the earth.

"I was more than a little intrigued with what Ben was sharing, so I got in touch with him at the high school and asked him to be on the show," said Andy.

"Good morning, Mr. Neverson," Andy said. "Thank you for agreeing to be on my show."

"Glad to be here, and please call me Ben. Everyone else does."

"I heard your presentation at the mayor's Planning Commission the other day, and I was intrigued. But first, tell me a little about yourself: where you grew up, what brought you to Link Lake for a job, and how you got interested in climate change. I'm sure you know there are a fair number of people who think climate change is a hoax."

Ben laughed. "Yes, but the vast majority of scientists believe it is much more than a hoax. I suspect a few people may be changing their minds about climate change after the flood you had here a few months ago.

"To your questions," Ben began, "I was born and grew up in Chicago. When I was a kid, my parents took my brothers and me on camping trips up here in Wisconsin, to our west, especially Yellowstone Park and several other places. I grew to love the outdoors and nature, and then, with my college studies, I began to learn how the environment was changing and what we, as human beings, are doing to cause that change. My research at the University of Illinois focused on climate change and alternative ways of helping to slow it down, if not stop it."

Andy said, "The mayor's commission has been thinking about energy and how the village and the surrounding area might become energy self-sufficient as one way of responding to climate change. They have been thinking about waterpower as an alternative, but as you know, they have dropped that idea. In fact, since the flood, the Planning Commission has turned its attention to how to increase employment opportunities in Link Lake, how to bring broadband here for better internet service, and how to improve Link Lake generally so more people would want to live here.

"More generally, the mayor was hoping the Planning Commission would help support countrywide activities, such as those related to alternative approaches to generating electricity that are more environmentally friendly than many that continue to be used today.

"The mayor asked Ben to share some of his research on geothermal energy as an alternative to coal and natural gas plants. Can you share a bit more of your thinking with our listeners?"

"Sure," said Ben. "First, the idea of geothermal energy is not new. The country of Iceland has been using it for many years and is a world leader. About 70 percent of Iceland's energy comes from geothermal resources. About 90 percent of the country's homes are heated with geothermal energy. In 2024, the U.S. had ninety-three power plants using geothermal energy.

"It works this way," Ben continued. "Huge drills reach deep into the earth until they reach underground reservoirs heated by the earth's crust. The resulting water vapor is brought to the surface and operates generators that create electricity. It is an excellent way of generating electricity with next to no environmental pollution."

"Ben, we are about out of time. Thank you so much for stopping by. I'm sure we'll be hearing more about your ideas.

"We close with what the old Norwegian says: 'It's hard to get from here to there if you are unclear about here and haven't thought much about there.'"

27
Fred and Oscar

The two old retired farmer friends pulled out the chairs at their reserved table at the Black Oak Café. Pauline was there ahead of them, ready to pour coffee as soon as they settled in.

"Well," Oscar said after taking a sip of coffee.

"Well, what?" said Fred rather gruffly.

"Well, what's new?" asked Oscar, smiling at his longtime friend.

"Finally got Bill Augustine's house fixed well enough so he could go back to living there. A flood can sure cause a lot of trouble," said Fred.

"So good of you to help him out," said Oscar. "He doesn't have a lot of friends in Link Lake, especially after he shot his mouth off at the recent community meeting."

"He needed help, so I helped him," said Fred. "Lots of people in Link Lake helped each other over the past few months."

They sat quietly for a few minutes, enjoying their breakfast of scrambled eggs and toast.

"That flood was really something," Fred said, finishing a piece of toast and rubbing his chin with a napkin.

"Sure was. Don't wanna see anything like that again," said Oscar. "By the way, did you listen to WLLK a couple of mornings ago?"

"Nope. I've been too busy helping Bill."

"Andy Dee, the radio guy, had been to one of the mayor's Planning Commission meetings—first time they've met since the flood."

"Andy's got an interesting program. I usually listen," said Fred.

"First thing he reported was the village is gonna repair the dam and make it stronger. And they also approved building a kind of levee along the lake with nearby homes to keep them from flooding," Oscar said.

"Sounds like good ideas. If the dam goes out, we're all gonna be in big trouble. A levee along the lake isn't a bad idea either. That will help protect the homes closest to the lake that suffered the most damage," Fred said.

"Andy also interviewed the new science teacher at the high school. Guy's been doing research on climate change, especially geothermal energy," Oscar said.

"So what in hell is geothermal energy?"

"You don't know what geothermal energy is?" said Oscar. "Tell you the truth, I never heard of it either."

"So what is it?" asked Fred.

"Heat energy from the earth."

"Heat energy from where?" asked Fred.

"From the earth," repeated Oscar.

"Thought that's what you said."

"This new science teacher said it was a form of energy that countries like Iceland have been using for years."

"Didn't know that," said Fred. "What's that got to do with Link Lake?"

"I suspect not much in the short run, but it's an idea for the country to consider," said Oscar.

"The country, huh? Seems to me Link Lake's got a bunch of its own problems, such as preventing floods and how to keep our high school graduates from leaving once they have finished their schooling," said Fred.

"True, but we've got to think about bigger things as well."

"Well, you just go ahead and think about bigger things. I've scarcely got time to think about the problems right here in our backyard."

28

Ben and Jackie Jo

Ben Neverson found himself stopping at the library several times a week after completing his work at the high school each day. His excuse was to do further reading about environmental issues, especially climate change, but the real reason was Jackie Jo Jensen. To use an old-fashioned term, he was smitten with her. Ben didn't know if her feelings were mutual, but he couldn't remember when he had such an attraction to someone.

Even though they both had apartments in the same house, they seldom saw each other there. Ben was extremely busy with his new job at Link Lake High, often leaving for school before seeing Jackie Jo, who left for the library a little before nine. Same in the evening. Ben was back in his apartment by five o'clock, while Jackie Jo was at events at the library until nine most evenings.

Ben stopped by the library on a Friday afternoon, checked the sign that reported upcoming activities, and noticed none were scheduled that evening. He proceeded to the checkout desk, where Jackie Jo was busy at work.

"Hi, Ben," Jackie Jo said, looking up from her work. He stood there a little longer than he usually did. "Something I can do for you?"

"As a matter of fact, yes," said Ben, working up enough courage to ask. "Would you like to go out to dinner with me tonight?"

"Sure," said Jackie Jo, wondering why this good-looking guy had taken so long to ask her for a date.

"I'll make reservations at the Silvercryst on Silver Lake. I've never been there but heard it's a nice place," said Ben. "Can I pick you up right after work?"

"Sure. But I need to stop by the apartment for a bit before we go," said Jackie Jo.

Promptly at five, Ben was in front of the library, sitting in his old Honda, wearing his "dressy" clothes, which consisted of a clean shirt and pants.

Five minutes later, Jackie Jo was in Ben's car, and they were on their way back to the Williams House. It was a clear, warm evening, with most trees showing off their early fall colors. Less than half an hour later, Jackie Jo was ready, wearing a blue dress, with her hair down and resting on her shoulders. At work, she always had her hair tied back.

When Jackie Jo got back into Ben's car, he could smell her heavenly cologne. He wanted to gather her in his arms and kiss her, but he didn't.

A half-hour later, they arrived at the Silvercryst. The parking lot was nearly filled with cars as it was Friday night, which meant fish fry night in most Wisconsin restaurants and supper clubs. Ben took Jackie Jo's hand, and they walked across the parking lot and soon stood by the check-in desk.

"We have reservations," Ben said and gave his name.

"Follow me," the fellow at the desk said as he led them to their table for two by the window that overlooked Silver Lake. After they were seated, he handed each of them a menu and asked, "What can I get you to drink?"

"I'll have some white wine," said Jackie Jo.

"Same for me," said Ben.

The evening couldn't have been more beautiful. A full moon was reflecting on the still waters of Silver Lake. One of the most beautiful sights one might see anywhere in Wisconsin.

They glanced at their menus. Jackie Jo pointed out the two fish specials and asked Ben if he knew about the long-standing Wisconsin tradition of fish on Friday night.

He said he wasn't aware of it. Jackie Jo admitted that she didn't know the reason other than this is what you'd expect to eat on Friday nights in Wisconsin.

"Wonderful view," Jackie Jo said as she looked out the window at the lake.

"Sure is," Ben said, looking back at his menu.

Their waiter arrived to take their orders. "Made up your mind?"

"I'll have the baked fish," said Jackie Jo, smiling.

"Same for me," said Ben.

Ben lifted his glass of wine. "Here's a salute to the Williams House and to Link Lake."

Jackie Jo lifted her wine glass and touched it to Ben's.

"Cheers," Jackie Jo said.

"So how do you like Link Lake and the high school?" Jackie Jo asked, changing the subject.

"Better than I expected. Bunch of sharp kids. Both boys and girls interested in science and in protecting the environment. I'm impressed and pleased. Teaching is a lot easier when the kids are interested in the subject."

"Of course, the recent flood is on everybody's mind. That's all the folks at the library want to talk about. Why it happened. What we can do to make sure it doesn't happen again," said Jackie Jo.

"That's the talk around the high school as well. Some of the materials used when the high school was an emergency shelter for flooded people are still there," said Ben. "A practical reminder of the flood."

For a few minutes they ate, enjoying their dinners and the view over Silver Lake.

"Want any more wine?" Ben asked.

"No, I'm good," said Jackie Jo.

"How about dessert? Anything?"

"Nope. Nothing more. But this was wonderful. Thanks for asking me. Sure beats eating my own cooking, sitting home in my apartment staring at the walls."

"Same here," said Ben, "except I'm betting your cooking is a lot better than mine." As he said it, he hoped he would have a chance to eat some of Jackie Jo's cooking.

With their meal and wine finished and another minute or two spent looking out over the lake, they left the restaurant, walked across the parking lot, and got into Ben's ancient car. Before he could start the engine, Jackie Jo slid over from the passenger seat and kissed Ben long and passionately.

"Thank you for this evening," Jackie Jo said. "Thank you so much." She kissed him again and cuddled next to him as they drove back to Link Lake—both with feelings they hadn't experienced in a long time.

29

Recall Election

Ames County Argus
"Recall Election Scheduled"

A recall election for Link Lake's mayor, Jon Jessup, is scheduled for the second Tuesday in November. Olaf Knudson, who had been Link Lake's mayor prior to Jessup's close win, has collected enough signatures for a recall election.

When announcing the upcoming recall election, Knudson said, "I really had been reelected at the last regular election when Jon Jessup won by a handful of crooked votes. A vote for me is a vote to return Link Lake to what it had been—a wonderful, close-knit community with low taxes and no foolhardy ideas for its future."

When contacted by the Argus for a comment, Mayor Jessup said it was a shame the village had to waste its time and money on a recall election when the village had so many problems that needed attention. He hoped that most of the Link Lake voters would vote for him so he and the hardworking Planning Commission could continue to work on details for the village's future.

Fred and Oscar pulled out the chairs at their reserved table at the café, which was nearly filled with customers on this chilly November morning.

"Well, he's done it," said Oscar, reaching for his cup of coffee that Pauline had recently filled. "The old bastard has done it."

"What old bastard has done what?" asked Fred, taking a big sip of his coffee.

"Old Olaf Knudson," answered Oscar.

"What's he done now? He's not mayor anymore," said Fred.

"You read the recent issue of the *Argus*?" asked Oscar.

"Can't say that I have," said Fred. "Just too darn busy doin' other stuff. Didn't take time to read the *Argus*."

"Well, you should read it."

"So now you tellin' me what I ought to be readin'," said Fred, a bit miffed by Oscar's suggestion.

"Fred, Fred," Oscar said, putting his hand on his old friend's arm. "I'm not trying to tell you what to read. The *Argus* has a story in it about the upcoming recall election. Old Olaf has gotten enough signatures on a petition, so there's gonna be a recall election. He is bound determined to have another vote. The old bugger believes he won the last election, and now he's gonna prove it with this recall election."

"He'll lose again," said Fred quietly. "A bunch of folks have come to like Jon Jessup and his new ideas. Just a few old-timers are holdin' out for Olaf."

"Problem is, all the work of the Planning Commission is on hold until after the election. I'm a member of that commission, as you know. Got a call from the mayor's office yesterday saying the commission won't be meeting until after the election. That's when I first learned that the recall election was going to happen," said Oscar.

The two old farmers continued with their breakfasts, not saying anything. Finally, Oscar said, "Fred, what's going on with this country? I thought the flood brought Link Lake people together, but now this recall election is going to tear us apart again. Just can't figure it out. Just can't." Oscar shook his head.

"I've known old Olaf Knudson for lots of years. We both went to Link Lake High School with him. I used to think he was a decent sort, but now he's pulling this 'I've been wronged' business. What's gotten into the guy? Why doesn't he just shut up and enjoy being retired, like we are doing?" said Fred.

"Fred, think about what you're saying. You aren't just sitting in your rocking chair and enjoying your retirement. You've been busy writing about Link Lake's history and doing it pretty well, I might add. And I'm busy on the mayor's Planning Commission," said Oscar.

"All true," said Fred. "But neither of us is looking for some 'power' position."

"I guess there is a difference between seeking power and simply helping out when asked," said Oscar.

"Gotta be careful with what you're sayin'," said Fred. "Just because you are old doesn't mean you can't be a leader. It's just that some older leaders, like Olaf, are stuck in the past and want us to stay there with him."

"One thing is surely true," began Oscar, taking a last sip of his coffee. "Link Lake has a bunch of old-timers living here, and just because they are old doesn't mean they can't make a difference in helping the community move forward. I would say each one of us, no matter how old we are, and if our health is halfway decent, should help our community move forward. There is lots of room for old-timers to volunteer—at the school, library and museum, at the health clinic. There is a lot to do, and we old-timers can help do it. The worst thing we can do is do nothing and allow our communities to wither away and die and eventually be forgotten."

30

Radio WLLK

"Good morning to all on this frosty morning. This is Andy Dee, your voice of reason, coming to you from WLLK in the heart of Link Lake, Wisconsin. Before we move to the news, and there is lots of it, we look in on Ole and Ollie and see what they are up to today.

"Walking downtown in Link Lake, both Ole and Ollie met a fellow who offered them a free lifetime membership in an organization. They both refused, saying that they didn't think they would live that long.

"The big news today is the upcoming recall election of our mayor, Jon Jessup. It will be held on the second Tuesday in November. Voters will have a choice between our current mayor, Jon Jessup, and our former, longtime mayor, Olaf Knudson. We will keep you informed of news leading to the recall election and, of course, the results.

"I've wanted to have Jackie Jo, the head librarian, on our show for some time. She has been so busy, but today she was free, and we have her here in the studio.

"Welcome, Jackie Jo," said Andy. "I am so pleased that you are able to be with us this morning."

"I'm glad to be here."

"So what's going on at the Increase Joseph Memorial Library?"

asked Andy. "I know about your writing class. Some great history writing is coming from that group. But what else?"

"Where do I begin? First off, our morning program for preschoolers, where I read books to them, is so much fun, and a few more kids are coming each time we meet.

"Our lunch program for seniors is a huge success. We just about fill every table in our community room. As you know, we have a goodly number of seniors living in Link Lake, and they not only enjoy the meals provided, but they have such a good time talking with each other."

"What about the regular stuff, like the number of books checked out?" asked Andy.

"Each month the numbers increase. Remember a few years ago when some folks were saying that public libraries were a thing of the past and would all close as people turned to their computers for what the library does now? Remember Mark Twain's words when he read his obituary in the paper? 'The reports of my death are greatly exaggerated.' The same thing can be said about public libraries; the report of their deaths is greatly exaggerated.

"I would argue that the public libraries are as important, and maybe even more important today than ever. One reason is that people like to get together with others. The library provides that opportunity. Our library is abuzz with people from the moment it opens in the morning until it closes in the evening."

"By the way," Andy asked with a big smile, "has your writing class gotten any more information about the 1940 bank robbery? All the old-timers still talk about it, especially the part about what happened to the money."

"Nope, they have not," said Jackie Jo. "They all talk about it, but no one wants to write about it." She still hadn't told anyone that she had found the money floating in the library basement. It was still in the library safe.

"Thank you for joining me this morning. We are out of time for now," said Andy. "We'll close with another of our famous old Norwegian sayings: 'If you can't jump over it, go around it.'"

31
Ben and Jackie Jo

Jackie Jo and Ben spent most Friday evenings visiting the restaurants and supper clubs in the area, trying out their fish fries. They were not disappointed. Their attraction toward each other seemed to grow with each outing, but something was missing. They both knew it but didn't talk about it. Each knew what they wanted.

On a recent Friday evening, Ben asked Jackie Jo if she could take off from work on the coming Saturday. He suggested driving north to see the fall colors. "One of my fellow teachers said fall was the most beautiful season in Wisconsin. Even better than summer. I'll make reservations for us at a motel near Rhinelander, a good place I've heard about."

Jackie Jo didn't ask if he had reserved two rooms, but she hoped it was only one.

Ben and Jackie Jo packed a few things, including a lunch. On Saturday morning, they were in Ben's Honda on their way to Plainfield, Interstate 39, and on their way north. Ben had checked his computer and learned it was about a two-hour drive to Rhinelander. The motel where he had made reservations was about five miles east of Rhinelander on Lake Thompson—a beautiful place he'd been told. Jackie Jo and Ben had not been farther north in Wisconsin than Link Lake, in central Wisconsin. Ben once checked, and it was nearly 250 miles from Link Lake to Ashland, which was located on Lake Superior.

Reaching Plainfield and Interstate 39, they drove past field after field of harvested potatoes, through what once had been Glacial Lake Wisconsin, formed when the glacier melted and retreated some ten thousand years ago. Once past Stevens Point and continuing north, they began to see what had once been an area filled with small dairy farms. Many of the old barns and silos were still in place, reminders of an earlier day when Wisconsin had thousands of small dairy farms scattered throughout much of the state, especially in central and southern Wisconsin. But the farther they drove north, the more the countryside changed from farmland to woodland, thousands of acres of trees, many of them maple, and most of them showing off their full fall wonder in colors from deep red to yellow.

They stopped at a roadside park located in a grove of maple trees in their full fall brilliance. No one else was in the park. "Oh, how beautiful those trees are," Jackie Jo said. She had enjoyed the fall colors in and around Link Lake, but none seemed as vivid as those in northern Wisconsin. There was not a cloud in the sky. It was bluer than either of them had ever known. The contrast of the trees' fall colors with the blue sky was something impossible for even the most talented artist to create, for surrounding the picture was the cleanest and purest of air—not a hint of air pollution. The wind was down, and the temperature had climbed into the sixties. A perfect day for a fall outing. A day for young lovers to discover the depth of their relationship.

They sat side by side on a park bench, slowly eating their lunch, and beyond enjoying the color all around them, they spent a good amount of time simply looking into each other's eyes.

Jackie Jo took Ben's hand and broke the silence. "Thank you so much for this day. It's just wonderful being here with you. I want you to know that. I've been looking forward to a weekend with you like this for a long time."

Ben smiled. "I felt this about you from the first day I met you, Jackie Jo, but I was so afraid I was the only one with those feelings. I was so afraid that you would say no when I asked you out that first time, when we went to the Silvercryst Supper Club. Such a wonderful night it was."

"Ben," Jackie Jo began, "I fell in love with you that night at the Silvercryst, but I didn't say it. I was afraid you didn't have the same feelings toward me."

Ben laughed. "Silly you. I wanted to say 'I love you,' too. But I was afraid to do it. There's an emotional side to me that's pretty fragile. So here goes, I love you, Jackie Jo."

She immediately wrapped her arms around Ben and kissed him.

After a bit, they were once more on their way to Rhinelander. They turned on Highway 8, a road through a mostly beautiful wooded area sprinkled with sparkling lakes. It was a beautiful drive. Soon they arrived at Rhinelander, where they were greeted by an enormous and strange-looking statue of an animal with a sign beneath it saying it was a hodag.

"What in the world is a hodag?" asked Jackie Jo.

"Beats me. Sure wouldn't want to meet one of those creatures," Ben said.

After driving a few miles east of Rhinelander, they reached their motel on Lake Thompson.

"Oh, what a beautiful location," Jackie Jo said as she got out of the car and looked across the blue waters of the lake. They gathered up their things and walked into the motel. The registration desk was only a few steps from the door.

"I have a reservation—Ben Neverson."

"Yes, we have you folks in room 208," said the clerk.

"By the way," Ben said, "a little while ago, we drove by this statue of a hodag. What in the world is a hodag?"

"Tell you what, stop down when you get settled in your room, and I'll give you the hodag story."

"Thanks," said Ben. "We just may do that."

"He didn't ask if we were married," Jackie Jo whispered as they walked to the elevator.

"No, he didn't," said Ben, smiling.

The room had an old-fashioned key that Ben used to open the door. Once inside, they were greeted with a fresh, clean smell.

"Nice place," Jackie Jo said, locking the door once they both were inside with their things.

"Wonder what stories this room has to tell?" asked Ben.

"Let's give it another story," said Jackie Jo as she pulled back the covers on the bed and began unbuttoning Ben's shirt. They spent the remainder of the afternoon enjoying the room, the view out the window, and each other. They came down for dinner, not remembering to ask for information about the hodag.

32
Radio WLLK

"Good morning, everyone. This is Andy Dee coming to you from WLLK-AM in downtown Link Lake, Wisconsin. If you haven't noticed, we are awash in fall color. It is that time of the year when Mother Nature gets out her paintbrush and has at it. We all benefit from her hard work creating the colors in this most beautiful of Wisconsin seasons.

"I'm sure you all have been patiently waiting and wondering what Ole and Ollie have been up to. Ole and Ollie had stopped by one of Link Lake's nearby apple orchards. They sat under a tree, enjoying one of the apples they picked. 'Do you know what?' asked Ole after taking a big bite from his apple.

"'No, what?' answered Ollie.

"'When you are eating an apple and come to a worm, be thankful it's not half a worm.'

"'I'll keep that in mind,' said Ollie as he continued to enjoy his big red apple and smiling from ear to ear.

"Let's leave those two old codgers to their apples and move on to something extremely important for Link Lake: Who should be our mayor?

"As you all know, we are holding a recall election here in Link Lake on the second Tuesday in November. Our former mayor, Olaf

Knudson, has gathered enough signers to hold a recall election, with him and our present mayor, Jon Jessup, on the ballot.

"It has been the policy of Radio WLLK not to back any one candidate for office. Our policy has been to inform our listeners about the various candidates running for a position and let the voters decide who should be the winner. But today, we are breaking our long-standing policy, and I am urging you to vote for our present mayor, Jon Jessup. I have Mayor Jessup here in the studio this morning.

"Good morning, Mayor. I know how busy you must be, but this upcoming election is no laughing matter."

"Thanks for asking me on your show. First, let me say, I'm extremely disappointed we are even having this recall election. I was elected fair and square—not by a lot of votes, but enough to win. The future of Link Lake is at stake."

"So why are we having a recall election in the first place? You do something wrong?"

The mayor laughed. "I don't think I did anything wrong. Our previous mayor is unhappy that I am doing some things right. Things he wouldn't think of doing."

"Such as?"

"We are working on a number of future-related things, but the flood forced everything to a stop. To tell you the truth, I was encouraged by how people came together during and after the flood. Everyone was helping everyone else. No one seemed concerned about who believed what or who they voted for in the last election. But, unfortunately, that's all changed. We're back to where we were, even further back than when I was first elected. We have managed to reinforce the dam so it won't go out and cause another flood like we had. We were just about to sign contracts for building a retaining wall alongside the lake, so when we have heavy rains like we recently had, it will not overflow. But that's now on hold."

"What about your Planning Commission?"

"Not meeting—lots of good ideas sitting there, waiting and hoping. Beyond fixing the dam, we've got several other things done. I'm sure you've seen the new greenhouses going up on the west side of Link

Lake. We've convinced a company that grows year-round vegetables to come here. We're about ready to have fresh-grown vegetables here in Link Lake year-round."

"That sounds like a good idea. I suspect the company also brought some new jobs to town."

"Yup, they did," said the mayor. "As I'm sure you've noticed, they also have installed a whole bunch of solar panels, enough to provide all the electricity they need for the greenhouses and some left over for the village to use."

"What next?"

"Well, if Olaf happens to win the recall election, these new ideas will grind to a halt. Jackie Jo knows I plan to add to her library budget the next go-round. If I lose the election, I'm sure that will not happen. We are working on repairing the village streets. That's been a problem for a lot of years; we were ready to do it. I doubt Olaf will approve much money for that."

"Frustrating, isn't it?"

"I'm darn sure Olaf will not be increasing any taxes. If anything, he'll likely want to cut some of them. That's what draws a lot of people to him. 'Keep them damn taxes low.' I fear for the future of our public library, our museum, our new cultural arts center in the old mercantile building, and our historical society. They are all gems with quite limited resources; we had hoped to help each of them a bit more. Above all, the Village of Link Lake has to deal with change. It's something each of us personally faces, and it's true for villages and cities as well."

"I'm sure you're right about that, and I agree with you when you said one time that we just can't sit here and wait for change to happen and then ignore it or adjust to it as best we can with the resources we have. We should be in charge of the changes we want, identify them, and then find the resources needed to make them happen. What about doing something about climate change?"

"Funny you should ask. We've both heard Olaf often say that there is no such thing as climate change. It's just another one of them hoaxes that wild-eyed liberals keep saying we must do something about. Olaf says, and often loudly: 'How in the world can we do something about something that doesn't exist?' When I mention the recent flood and how it was likely the result of climate change—because nothing as powerful as that flood has ever come to beat down on Link Lake—he just smiles. Weather happens. Rains happen. Blizzards happen, and yes, the occasional flood happens. It's the way it has always been; it's the way it will always be. The good Lord is in charge. We should quit messing with things we have nothing to do with."

Andy pointed at the clock on the wall. "We're about out of time. Thank you for being on the show this morning, and good luck with the coming election."

"Thanks, Andy. I very much appreciate being on your show."

"We close this segment with what that famous old Norwegian has to say: 'When you are doing nothing, how do you know when you are finished?'"

33

Fred and Oscar

The two old farmers sat at their reserved table at the café, sipping on their coffee and waiting for their breakfast of eggs sunny-side up with toast. Once, when Pauline offered to serve Oscar scrambled eggs, he said, "Don't like my eggs messed up that way. I like them yellow yolks staring back at me. They wake me up."

Fred finally broke the silence. "So, Oscar, what's goin' on with you?"

"Hate to say it this way," said Oscar, "but everything is going on, and nothin' is goin' on."

"Well, that's a pretty darn complicated set of words if I ever heard them. How can somethin' be goin' on when nothin' is going on?"

"Well, that's pretty much how I see the world this morning," said Oscar. "Pretty much the way I see it." Oscar took another long sip of coffee. Pauline arrived with their breakfast of eggs sunny-side up with toast, butter, and homemade jelly.

When Fred was nearly finished with his breakfast, he said, "So you gonna tell me what's in your craw this morning—somethin's stuck there all right. Stuck tight from the look of them deep furrows in your forehead."

"You listen to WLLK this morning? That fellow Andy Dee has an interesting program."

"Didn't have time to do it. Had an assignment from the writing class. You know, that Jackie Jo is some kind of teacher. Never thought she'd get us old-timers to do anything, especially writing. But here I am, scribbling down my stories—stuff I hadn't thought about for years. Now I'm gettin' it down on paper," Fred said.

"So back to what's givin' you grief on this chilly sunny morning. The old Norwegian say somethin' you didn't agree with?"

"Nothin' to do with the old Norwegian or with Ole and Ollie, for that matter. What's in my craw is the upcoming recall election. Andy Dee had Mayor Jessup on his radio show this morning. The mayor is concerned that Olaf Knudson may win and be our mayor again."

"I can't believe old Olaf is doing this. The guy's old, is in his eighties, and has heart problems, I'm told. You'd think he'd want to do something other than deal with the problems Link Lake faces these days," said Fred.

"I thought it was just plain dumb of him to push for a recall election. Frankly, I don't think it was his idea. He has a bunch of buddies who pushed him to do this. There's a bunch people here in Link Lake who want the village to be like it was in the 1950s. They are the ones pushing for the recall," said Oscar.

"Expect you are right about that. I've known Olaf for a long time. He did a decent job when he was mayor. But things have changed a lot in the past thirty years. Now we are considering some new ideas, some new ways of thinking, thanks to Jon Jessup. I've been pretty impressed with Jon and what he's been able to do since he was elected," said Fred.

"What bothers me is this," said Oscar. "When the flood came washing through Link Lake, filling more than a few basements, and nearly wiping out the dam at the lake and causing more problems, people came together to help each other, not caring who voted for who. I thought the village had come together in a way we hadn't seen in years as people argued about nearly everything from taxes to why we should continue to have a library."

"Yup, you got it right," said Fred. "I can't figure out what's going on either. It's just weird. But I think Jon Jessup's going to win the election and win big. The village is headed in the right direction, with Jon Jessup leading."

"I hope you're right," said Oscar. "Sure hope so. I can't imagine what will happen to Link Lake if he loses. Just can't think about that."

34
Ben and Jackie Jo

Back from their outing to the north, and to their jobs at the high school and the Increase Joseph Memorial Library, it was difficult for the young couple to focus on their work as they recalled the fun they had on the trip, and much more. Now they knew for sure that they were clearly in love.

On Friday evening, they were once more at the Silvercryst Supper Club on Silver Lake, enjoying the fish fry, the remaining fall colors, and each other's company.

"So how was your week?" asked Ben as he took her hands in his.

"Just great," answered Jackie Jo. "Well, almost great."

"Why the 'almost'?" asked Ben.

"Well, first off, I can't get my mind off of you and the wonderful time we had up north. I'm happy about all that has happened and continues to happen at the library, especially the writing class that has done so much better than I thought it would."

"So what's the 'almost'?" asked Ben once more.

"The recall election that's coming soon," said Jackie Jo. "I can't imagine Mayor Jon Jessup losing. If he loses, I fear for the library and, frankly, my job. Olaf Knudson has no love for libraries. Do you know that he has not once been in our library for all the time I've been here?"

"As you know, I'm on the mayor's Planning Commission. We are on hold, not meeting until after the election. If Olaf wins, I'm sure there will be no more Planning Commission," said Ben.

"You've got that right. I've got something else I've been thinking about," Jackie Jo said, smiling. She finished her glass of wine.

"And that would be?" said Ben.

"What would you think about this?" Jackie Jo began. "We each have an apartment at the Williams House."

"Yes," replied Ben.

"We seem to like each other," Jackie Jo said.

"More than that," said Ben, smiling. He wondered where this conversation was going.

"What do you say . . ." Jackie Jo hesitated. "What do you say you come live with me in my apartment and we move you out of yours? You can get used to my cooking."

Ben took Jackie Jo in his arms and kissed her. "That's my answer."

"Now we've got to tell our landlord, and she may not be too keen on our idea. Folks of her generation would say that 'they are living in sin' when an unmarried couple moves in together."

"And she may be a little worried that she will lose the rent from one of her apartments," said Ben.

"That's true," said Jackie Jo, "but I don't really think she needs the money. Besides, she should be able to find another renter without too much trouble."

"So how should we handle this?" asked Ben.

"Well, let's meet with Emily tonight and tell her our plans. If she wants to kick both of us out, we'll find another place to live. That shouldn't be too hard."

It was about six o'clock in the evening when Jackie Jo and Ben arrived at the door of Emily's first-floor apartment at Williams House. Ben rang the doorbell. He soon heard footsteps, and then the door opened. "Hello, what can I do for you?" Emily said, wondering what the young couple had on their minds and if something had gone wrong in their apartments.

"May we come in?" asked Jackie Jo.

"Sure, come on in. She led them into the small parlor just off the dining room. Emily's apartment was slightly larger than Jackie Jo's and Ben's. The parlor had wallpaper with big orange flowers, something that Jackie Jo couldn't remember ever seeing before.

"Something need fixing?" Emily asked. That was the main reason her renters stopped by to talk.

"Nope, nothing like that. Everything works fine."

Emily had a puzzled look on her face. Had she done something wrong to offend them?

"I don't quite know where to start," said Jackie Jo. "Ben, you join in whenever you'd like," she said, looking at him. Sitting in a big stuffed chair and folding and unfolding his hands, he looked more than a little uncomfortable.

Now Emily looked even more concerned. What was going on that these two wanted to share with her? She had been preparing her supper when they arrived, and the smells of supper cooking seeped into the little parlor.

"Let me get right to it," said Jackie Jo. "I've asked Ben to live with me in my apartment."

"You what?" said Emily in a quiet voice.

"We are in love, and we want to live together," said Jackie Jo, smiling. She glanced at Ben, who was blushing.

"Let me see if I have this straight," said Emily. "You, Ben, want to move out of your apartment and move in with Jackie Jo. That right?"

"Yes, that's right. We like it here and are hoping you will let us do that."

"You realize what folks will say when they hear what you are doing, don't you? You both have important jobs. They expect men and women living together to be married."

"What will they say?" asked Jackie Jo, clearly wondering why the good folks of Link Lake cared what its young professionals were doing.

"They will say you are living in sin. How will you answer them when they say that?"

Without waiting a moment, Jackie Jo said, "I'll tell them we are living in love."

Ben said not a word but smiled from ear to ear.

Emily had a perplexed look on her face. She remembered hearing of a few people doing this, but it wasn't common. She remembered from way back hearing that her mother had done something like this, thus the reason for Emily's existence.

"Why don't you get married and solve the problem?" Emily suggested.

"We are not ready to get married," Jackie Jo said, looking at Ben and smiling.

Everything was quiet in the room, save for the *tick-tock* of an old windup clock on the wall.

"It will be okay," Emily said. "I like both of you—like you a lot. Go ahead and move in with each other. I won't tell anyone what you've done, but knowing this town, some wag will learn about it and then spread the word. I can tell you both don't care who knows about it. Bless you both. Can I offer you a cup of coffee?"

"No thanks," said Jackie Jo. "Ben and I are eating supper in my apartment in a little while. After supper, we'll start moving some of his things into my apartment. Thank you so much for agreeing to do this."

Ben and Jackie Jo left Emily's apartment and walked up to Jackie Jo's.

"So what's for supper?" Ben asked, learning for the first time that Jackie Jo was preparing it.

"You'll find out soon enough." Jackie Jo kissed Ben on the cheek.

"What's for dessert?" asked Ben, with a mischievous look.

"You'll find out soon enough," said Jackie Jo as she began preparing supper.

35

Recall Election

The second Tuesday in November dawned cool and frosty. As the old-timers would say, "There was frost on the pumpkins." Frost covered everything—the grass, the sidewalks, the roadways. The Village of Link Lake looked forward to the recall election with considerable fear and trepidation. They'd had no experience with a recall election. A good many of the residents of the village couldn't believe it was even happening. Mayor Jon Jessup won the election. Olaf Knudson lost, albeit by only a few votes. Nonetheless, he was the village's elected mayor. Why try to get rid of him when he's just getting started with several new ideas? So you don't like some of his ideas. Vote someone else in during the next mayoral election. Don't fuss around with a recall election to try and get rid of the mayor sooner than waiting until his term in office is up.

Campaign signs dotted a few lawns around the village. Simple signs, some of them homemade: "Vote Olaf Knudson" and "Vote Mayor Jon Jessup." Most people in town knew who they would vote for; they didn't need a sign to remind them.

The Increase Joseph Memorial Library was the only polling place in town and had been since it first opened. Jackie Jo arrived at the library at seven-thirty the morning of the recall election. People could start voting at eight o'clock. Stored away in one of the library's closets was a big sign with big red letters: "Vote Here." Jackie Jo dragged it outside and set it up on the library lawn. It wasn't needed. But someone had told Jackie Jo that the law required them to have the sign on the lawn.

By now, the poll workers, Carolyn Stevens, chair of the library board, and Emily Higgins, head of the Link Lake Historical Society, had the voting table set up in the library's reading room. The voting would be done on paper ballots and stuffed into a box labeled "Completed Ballots Here." Link Lake did not have any of those fancy electronic machines that automatically counted the votes. The two women who had been poll workers for many years were ready, hoping everything would go smoothly. They had read about fights at polling places, people yelling at each other, and even threats with guns. This had never happened at any elections held at Link Lake, and they hoped it never would. Carolyn and Emily had asked the village marshal to be on call, in case his services were needed. He'd said that after he finished voting, which would be sometime in mid-morning, he would plan to stay at the library, at least until noon, to make sure there was no trouble.

At a quarter to eight, the first voters arrived, and by eight, a line had formed outside the door and around the corner. Voting began exactly at eight. People showed their IDs to Carolyn, followed by Emily handing them a ballot and a pencil. They marked the ballot, folded it in half, stuffed it in the ballot box, and left. There was almost no discussion as people stood in line. It was a strange kind of silence, as Link Lake people were accustomed to talking with each other.

Jackie Jo watched all of this from her place behind the library counter. The first thing she observed was that a fair number of people in line were not regular library patrons. She'd never seen many of them in the library checking out a book, looking at some reference material, attending a meeting, doing the things library patrons do in a public library.

The second unspoken thing was how many people were probably wondering who everyone else was voting for. Jackie Jo had heard several library patrons asking why they were having an election. A few people stopped by Jackie Jo's desk to say hello, comment on the weather, or check out a book after voting.

Only three people were in line by nine o'clock when the polls were to close. Jackie Jo recognized them as people living in Link Lake but had jobs in Stevens Point. The polls closed, Jackie Jo dragged the big "Vote Here" sign back into the library and pushed it into a closet, where it would wait for the next election.

She left for home, leaving the poll workers with the onerous task of counting the votes, one at a time, and recording the results. After checking them twice, they called Andy Dee at WLLK with the results. Carolyn Stevens alerted Andy earlier that she would call when they finished the count. Andy had been regularly announcing that he would have the election results as soon as the votes were counted. Carolyn put in the call and informed Andy which of the two men had won the election.

36

Election Results

"This is Andy Dee at radio station WLLK breaking into our regular programming for news of the recall election for mayor of Link Lake, which was held today. I have just gotten a call from the poll workers over at Increase Joseph Memorial Library that the votes for the recall election have been counted—in fact, counted twice to make sure there were no errors. With fifty votes, the winner is Olaf Knudson, our previous mayor. We will be broadcasting Olaf's acceptance speech live thirty minutes from now. He will be speaking in the community room of the Increase Joseph Memorial Library."

Thirty Minutes Later – Increase Joseph Memorial Library

The community room was filled with people waiting to hear from their former mayor. Some were surprised that he had won the recall election and were concerned about the future of the Village of Link Lake. Others were pleased that they were returning to the quiet and careful leadership of Olaf Knudson, with his style of keeping taxes low and keeping wild, new ideas for the community under wraps.

Olaf Knudson arrived a bit late, accompanied by his wife, who helped him onto the little stage. At the podium, Adolph Gutzman, owner of the Link Lake Tap and leader of the group that organized the recall election, began speaking.

"Thank you all for coming out on this chilly but joyous evening. We are once more going to have our rightful mayor, Olaf Knudson, back in the mayor's office at the village hall."

The majority of the crowd broke into raucous cheering and applause. There was a sizable group, not enough to win a recall election, which supported Mayor Jessup. They quietly waited to hear what Olaf Knudson had to say and worried about the future of Link Lake.

Olaf held up his hands to quiet the audience. He stood slightly slumped over, with some of his snow-white hair slipping down over his right eye. With one hand, he pushed it back in place. He began to speak softly and quietly. Someone in the front row of the audience pointed to the microphone and said in a loud voice, "Speak closer to the mike, Olaf."

Once more, Olaf began, "My fellow citizens of Link Lake." Again the audience broke into loud applause and cheering. Olaf let them go on for a bit before holding up his arms to signal to stop so he could speak.

Speaking slowly, Olaf began, repeating, "My fellow citizens of Link Lake, it is my distinct . . . honor to thank those of you . . . who voted for me to be once more . . . your mayor."

Another round of applause and cheering. Jackie Jo and Ben sat in the back of the room. Ben whispered to Jackie Jo, "Did you know how much Link Lake folks liked their former mayor?"

"I surely didn't," whispered Jackie Jo. "This sounds like a love fest for the old guy. He doesn't look very healthy to me."

"He surely doesn't," whispered Ben.

Oscar Anderson and Fred Russo also sat in the back of the room, quietly listening and watching. Occasionally, they looked at each other and shook their heads, not saying anything.

Olaf once more began speaking. "I'm sorry . . . that Link Lake has been off . . . the track for . . . the past several months. Our present mayor . . . Jon Jessup should never have . . . been elected." Olaf stopped speaking, took a drink of water from the glass near the podium.

"Jon Jessup . . . is not a bad man, he . . . just doesn't understand us. He has . . . wild ideas. I'll make sure they are . . . squashed like a rotten tomato is squashed."

Loud clapping from the audience.

"I'm thinking . . . of this . . . Planning Commission . . . he organized. It . . . it has got to go."

More clapping.

"Have you . . . seen those weird . . . greenhouses . . . just west of town? Jessup invited that group to build and sell greenhouse-raised . . . vegetables. Who wants . . . to eat . . . greenhouse vegetables? That outfit . . . has got to go," said Olaf, his voice now slightly stronger than when he first began speaking.

"And that's . . . not all." Olaf took another drink of water and pushed back the strands of white hair that kept falling over his right eye. "This greenhouse outfit has erected a field full of . . . those damned solar panels. What an eyesore . . . they are. Who needs them? Link Lake surely doesn't.

"One more thing. A big thank you . . . to everyone . . . who turned out and helped those caught . . . in the recent flood. Weather people . . . assured us that the flood was . . . a hundred-year event. We won't . . . be seeing anything like that . . . for a good long time. What's Jon Jessup doing? He's about to . . . approve a contract . . . to build a retaining wall alongside the lake . . . where it ran over and contributed . . . to the flood. I'll . . . immediately put a stop to that. Such a wall . . . is expensive . . . and surely is not needed. One more way to keep our taxes low. "Well, I've said . . . enough. Thanks to everyone who . . . voted for me. I see a bright future ahead of us . . . being what we were . . . not what somebody thinks . . . we ought to be."

Olaf stepped back from the podium and waved his arm at the crowd. His wife took his elbow and helped him down from the little stage in front of the community room. A sizable number of people in the crowd jumped to their feet, clapping and cheering. Several others got up and left the room with disappointment on their faces.

37
Fred and Oscar

The following Monday found Fred and Oscar at their usual table in the Black Oak Café. They arrived at the same time, which was rare for them, as one was usually a few minutes late.

"So what do you think, Fred?" Oscar said as he hung his jacket on the back of his chair.

"About what?"

"About the future of Link Lake?" replied Oscar with a straight face.

"That's too big a topic for my aging mind to consider," said Fred.

"Well, you'd better begin thinking about it."

"Why is that?"

"Because the village is on its way toward going to hell," said Oscar.

"What was that you just said?" asked Fred, who put down his coffee and looked straight at his old friend.

"I said the Village of Link Lake is in big trouble," said Oscar.

"I think you said something about the village going to hell," said Fred. "Why don't you just say you are not happy that old Olaf Knudson won the recall election and will be back in the mayor's chair? I'm not very happy about that either."

"Fred, whatever words you might use, I'm worried about the future of Link Lake. Jon Jessup had us both looking back and looking ahead. Old Olaf has his eyes closed. He's not looking at anything except keeping taxes low. When he was mayor before, I never heard him talk about one new idea for the village. He simply sat in that big leather chair at the village hall and watched Link Lake slip backward. And whether he knows it or not, we have slipped backward. The cheese factory closed. The gristmill closed. The clothing store is gone. The lumberyard is gone. The train is gone and the tracks torn up. The hotel and drugstore are gone. No more car dealership."

"That's right," said Fred. "The Village of Link Lake is surely not what it was back in the fifties and sixties. When family farms disappeared, the village nearly disappeared as well. Something else has also disappeared."

"What's that?" Oscar said.

"Hope has disappeared," said Fred.

"The Village of Link Lake has lost its hope."

38
Ben and Jackie Jo

Jackie Jo and Ben finished moving his things into her apartment. A couple of nights after the recall election, they sat opposite each other at the kitchen table, eating dinner and enjoying each other's company.

"Looks like your stuff and my stuff seem to be getting along," Jackie Jo said, breaking the silence.

"Yes, it does," said Ben. "And that's not all that's getting along." Ben reached across the table and took Jackie Jo's hands in his. "We seem to be hitting it off pretty well, too."

Jackie Jo smiled and said, "You've noticed."

"I sure have," said Ben. "I don't think I've ever been happier."

"Nor I."

They sat quietly enjoying their meal when Ben broke the silence.

"What'd you think about the results of the recall election?"

"I don't want to think about it. It's the most devastating thing that could happen to Link Lake right now. Just when it is still recovering from a massive flood and doing some good basic planning under Jon Jessup's leadership, everything will come to a stop."

"You've got that right. I've been impressed with the mayor's Planning Commission. We've been discussing a bunch of new ideas—both to help Link Lake and to help the environment. One of the first things old Olaf said he would do is eliminate the Planning Commission," said Ben.

"I'm worried about the future of the library as well," Jackie Jo said. "Someone remembered when he was mayor before that one of his goals was to close the library. That person heard him say, 'Libraries are not needed anymore. If you want information, you go to the internet.' I don't think Olaf has ever been in the book part of the library. He has only attended meetings in the community room. Sad times. We've gotten so many things going at the library, including the Saturday writing class, which has turned out so much better than I thought it would."

They both sat quietly, finishing dinner. Jackie Jo looked at Ben. "I've got something I'd like to tell you, but it's a secret and not to be shared with anyone else," Jackie Jo began.

"A secret, huh? Something about you that you haven't shared with me, such as being in jail when you were younger?"

Jackie Jo laughed. "I have not been in jail, and this secret is not really about me, but in another way it is."

"Now you've got me interested," said Ben. "I like secrets."

"This is a serious secret," said Jackie Jo quietly. "Did anybody tell you about the bank robbery that took place here in 1940?"

"Yeah, I remember somebody on the school board took me aside and told me the story, sort of like this was the most important thing that ever happened in the history of Link Lake."

"Did this person share the punch line question, which apparently has been on the minds of the old-timers here in Link Lake since 1940?" asked Jackie Jo.

"If he did, I don't remember what it was," said Ben.

"The question was, 'After the bank robbery, what did the robber do with the money?'"

"I guess he did mention that, come to think of it," said Ben.

"A bunch of old-timers here in Link Lake firmly believe that somebody here in the village has the money," said Jackie Jo.

"So nobody knows who has the money?" said Ben.

"I know," said Jackie Jo quietly.

"You know?" Ben had a confused look on his face. "You know who has the money, and you haven't told anybody?"

"That's right," said Jackie Jo, "and I'm going to tell you, and it's a secret."

"So who has the money?" Ben asked.

"I do."

"Wait a minute, I'm confused. You say you have the bank money and haven't told anyone."

"I'm telling you," Jackie Jo said. She went on to explain how she had found the money in a bank bag floating in the water that half filled the library's basement during the flood. "It had been tucked away there and became dislodged with the floodwater. The words 'Link Lake Bank' were printed on the bag."

"How much money was there?" Ben asked, now more than a little interested in Jackie Jo's secret.

"Fifty thousand dollars," said Jackie Jo quietly.

"Whoa, that's a bunch of money," said Ben. "What are you going to do with it?"

"Right now, I've got it locked in the library's safe. I'm the only one with the combination. So far, you are the only one I've told about this."

Ben rubbed his chin. "I can think of a bunch of ways to spend fifty grand."

"I'm sure you can, but I've been thinking of using the money to make improvements in the library. With the old mayor back in office, I'm sure the library could use the money. But I don't know how to do it. The money is all in paper bills. I can't just peel off a few thousand and buy something for the library. Whoever I buy something from will wonder how I got so much cash and might even call the police. I just don't know what to do," said Jackie Jo.

"We'll figure something out." Ben took her hand. "We'll figure something out."

"I'll bet you didn't know this little secret either—it's really not much of a secret," said Jackie Jo.

"What?" asked Ben, with a surprised look on his face.

"Our landlord, Emily, is the bank robber's daughter.

She and Ethyl at the library are twins. Their mother was quite taken by the bank robber, and guess what? Nine months after he was captured, Ethyl and Emily were born," said Jackie Jo.

"Well, I'll be," said Ben. "Link Lake does have an interesting history."

"I suspect we don't know the half of it," said Jackie Jo.

Ben changed the subject. "Have you heard the weather report?"

"I have not," said Jackie Jo. "Another storm coming our way?"

"That's what the weather people are saying. They don't know how strong it will be, but they are concerned."

39

Tornado

It was a warm spring afternoon. Jon Jessup stood on the porch of his Link Lake home, still smarting a bit from his loss in the recent recall election. His wife, Amy, stood next to him. Her law office was in their home, and she had no appointments this morning. Their house stood on a little hill, and they, along with their close neighbors, had little damage from the recent rains and flood.

"Still fretting about your election loss, Jon?" she said, taking his hand and looking into his eyes. "You were a good mayor—apparently too good for Link Lake."

"I just can't believe I lost," Jon said. "The Planning Commission was developing some really good ideas for the town. The writing class at the library dug up Link Lake history, which was new to lots of people. We had a lot going for us, and I wrongly thought the town was behind me—they did vote for me at the last election."

"The majority of folks here are afraid of change. They claim to like things just as they are," said Amy. "That's why they voted Olaf back in as mayor."

"But don't they realize the town is changing rapidly? Link Lake is not anything like it was back in the fifties and sixties," said Jon.

"Most folks seem to trust Olaf Knudson to help them avoid change and keep their taxes low. Keep the taxes low is top priority," said

Amy, her long blonde hair gently blowing as a breeze came up from the west.

"Did you listen to the weather report this morning?" asked Amy.

"I did not. What did you hear?"

"The weather bureau has issued a weather advisory for a possible tornado headed our way. You'd best tune in the weather radio and hear for yourself," said Amy.

"Not another storm," said Jon. "Link Lake has had its share of weather events."

In a few minutes, Jon returned to the porch, where Amy waited and continued to watch the western sky. "What did you learn?" Amy asked.

Jon held the weather radio so both could hear: "Attention, Attention, storm warning. A tornado has touched down in western Ames County and is headed for Link Lake," the weather person said. "Seek shelter immediately."

They watched the town's police car slowly drive by on the street below their home. They heard the police car's speaker intoning, "Tornado warning. Tornado warning. Find shelter immediately."

Just then, they heard their weather radio beeping and rushed into the house to hear the message: "This is a tornado warning for the residents of Link Lake. Take shelter in your basement away from a wall, or if you are in a downtown area, seek out the nearest storm shelter," a professional-sounding voice said. The warning repeated.

"Wouldn't that be something if a tornado hit Link Lake just when we got things mostly back together after the flood," said Jon.

Before heading for their basement, Jon and Amy glanced outside once more. They watched a wall of thick black clouds building ever higher in the west and tumbling over each other as lightning bolts shot out of them, followed by ever louder thunderclaps. Then they saw the tail of the tornado touch down west of Link Lake, followed by a huge cloud of dust and debris. They immediately hurried to their basement, taking with them their battery-operated weather radio and cell phones. The police car they had seen earlier had disappeared, no doubt looking for a safe place to avoid the tornado.

When the public buildings in Link Lake were constructed, each building, such as the high school, the village hall, and the public library, had rooms in their basements designed as storm shelters, but they had never been used. A couple of them had flooded, including the one at the Link Lake Memorial Library and the one at the village hall. But these shelters had dried sufficiently since the flood and were now filling with people running from the downtown businesses. WLLK was continuously broadcasting. "Emergency: A tornado has been spotted but minutes from downtown Link Lake. Those with friends at the Link Lake Tap or eating at the Black Oak Café should immediately rush to one of the nearby storm shelters at the high school, village hall, or the library."

Long lines of people were rushing down Main Street toward the storm shelters. Some people chose to jump in their cars and race out of town, trying to escape before the tornado arrived. Those rushing to one of the tornado shelters could see the massive funnel cloud coming their way. Even more frightening, they could hear it. It sounded like a train roaring into town. But it was no train; it was a menacing twisting wind, sometimes reaching a hundred miles per hour and more at ground level. As the black funnel cloud moved along the ground at about twenty miles an hour, it smashed and picked up everything in its path. If people arriving at the storm shelter looked toward the western sky, they would see trees, picnic benches, roofing materials, cooking grills, all spinning around, and the debris causing destruction when it crashed into something.

As it was a warm Saturday afternoon, the library had been nearly filled with kids, their parents, and several regular library customers. Ben Neverson was there reading books about climate change. Jackie Jo and Ethyl were busy and did not have a radio on. They didn't hear the tornado warning until one of the library customers rushed into the library, yelling, "Tornado, tornado!" With Ben's help, Jackie Jo quickly moved around the library alerting patrons of the tornado and pointing them toward the stairway to the storm shelter in the basement.

When Jackie Jo and Ben were sure that everyone was downstairs, they, with the sound of the massive tornado in their ears, hurried to the storm shelter, which still smelled musty from the flood months before. Jackie Jo glanced over to the far wall, where the safe with the stolen money was. It hadn't moved. Soon the sound of a roaring freight train became ever louder, and the library's walls seemed to shake a bit. Jackie Jo heard the sound of breaking boards and immediately wondered how the library was faring as the funnel cloud continued down Main Street. Jackie Jo and Ben sat on the floor in front of the little black safe, arms around each other, as they waited out the storm. They didn't have to wait long. One minute, there was the sound of breaking boards and a freight train, and a few minutes later, there was quiet—extreme quiet. They, and everyone else in the dark storm shelter, sat quietly waiting. Then they heard someone opening the stairway door and shouting down the stairs, "It's safe to come out now. The tornado has passed," a voice said.

40
Storm Damage

Radio station WLLK managed to stay on the air during the storm; they had a generator providing power. Also, the station building was half a mile off Main Street and suffered no damage from the twister.

"This is Andy Dee, your radio host, coming to you from stormy Link Lake, Wisconsin. So far we've been lucky to continue on the air and provide blow-by-blow stories of what this recent tornado has done to our village. Some of our residents have fled in their cars. We hope they successfully outran the storm. Most of you hunkered down in your basements or found your way to one of our several storm shelters. I hope to have a report soon on the extent of the storm damage.

"Matt Higgins, deputy sheriff and husband of our new cultural arts center executive director in the remodeled mercantile building, is here with a report. Thanks for stopping by, Matt. How bad is the damage?"

"Pretty bad," Matt answered. "The tornado came right down Main Street and leveled several buildings in its path. Let's see, I'm sure I don't have all the ones that are gone. Each one leveled to the ground includes Spranger Hardware, the Black Oak Café, and the Link Lake Tap—there may be others. The mercantile, now our cultural arts center, still stands strong. The Increase Joseph Memorial Library was hit, but all I could see so far was part of the roof missing.

The high school is far enough from Main Street, so I'm told it has next to no damage. And the Church of Peace wasn't touched. A goodly number of homes near Main Street were leveled. So far, there are no deaths or reports of serious injuries."

Back at the mike, Andy said, "Everyone remembers that the Link Lake High School had been a shelter and feeding center for those who had water damage from the recent flood. They are preparing to do the same for those who lost their homes to the tornado. I have been in touch with the power company, and they couldn't tell me how long it would be before the power is back on. They did say to be careful if you see a downed power wire—don't try to move it. It may be live."

Jon Jessup and his wife, Amy, continued to listen to radio reports on their battery-operated radio. They had come upstairs from the safety of their basement and were now looking down on Link Lake's Main Street, which looked like pictures of war scenes.

"This is a terrible thing to say," began Jon as he rubbed his chin, "but I'm happy I'm not mayor now. Olaf is gonna have his hands full, working to put Link Lake back together again. We'd just about gotten over the flood a while back and now a tornado. I wonder what he thinks about climate change now."

41
Fred and Oscar

A Week Later in Willow River

"Well, I see you finally found it," said Oscar to his old friend, Fred.

"Made a wrong turn. Not used to driving in these big cities," Fred said, smiling.

"Well, glad you found it. Not the same as the Black Oak Café. I'm gonna miss that place."

"So will I," said Fred. "I suspect we'll have to get used to the 'Country Cooking Restaurant,' not a very original name.

How's the coffee?"

"Don't know. Haven't had any yet."

Just then, a perky young blonde waitress appeared at their table with a big smile, a coffee pot, and two cups.

"You gents interested in some coffee?" she asked.

They both agreed that they were. She set down the cups and poured their coffee.

"You ready to order yet?" she asked, pointing to the menus in front of them. "By the way, where are you from? I haven't seen you here before."

"Link Lake," said Oscar. "We live on farms just outside of Link Lake."

"Oh my gosh. It's just awful what happened to Link Lake. My husband and I drove over there yesterday. Not much left of the place. Especially the downtown businesses. Gone, completely gone," she said.

"Yup, lots of damage," said Fred. "Just like some of those towns in Oklahoma that were destroyed by tornadoes with merely a pile of trash left. Nobody seriously hurt in Link Lake. But we did have one casualty, our newly elected mayor, from a recall election, Olaf Knudson. He had gone to the storm shelter in the village hall along with everyone else in the building. He had a heart attack at the same time the tornado was roaring through. He hadn't been well, was in his eighties, and I guess the shock of it all was just too much for him."

"I'm so sorry," the young waitress said.

"The village gonna rebuild? I've never seen such a mess, such total destruction."

"Sure," Oscar said. "Village has a great, interesting history."

"Let me know when you are ready to order," the waitress said as she walked away, her sunny smile gone.

"You know, Fred," said Oscar. "She asks a good question. I can't imagine the village not rebuilding. The folks in Link Lake, with all of their faults, really love their town and will work hard to bring it back. I'm sure they will."

"I was pleased to hear that the new cultural arts center took a direct hit from the tornado and suffered only a couple of broken windows. That's one tough old building, especially since it was remodeled," said Fred.

"The library took a glancing blow. Tornado took off some of its roof," Oscar said. "I noticed it had a big hunk of blue canvas covering the hole in the roof. Jackie Jo and her boyfriend, Ben, rode out the storm in the library's storm shelter, along with the library customers who were there at the time."

"I heard something else, too," said Fred.

"And that would be?"

I heard that Jackie Jo has started a fund drive to raise money to repair the roof damage, but also to add a new children's reading room and a new computer center."

"Really," said Oscar.

"I stopped by the library yesterday and asked Jackie Jo about that. She showed me the handout describing the fund drive. She said that she had already gotten a sizable grant from an anonymous donor. So she's optimistic that we will have a larger, improved Increase Joseph Memorial Library in Link Lake," said Fred.

"Talking about money," Oscar began, "I haven't heard anybody recently ask about what happened to the 1940 bank robbery money."

"I haven't heard a word either. People have been too busy worrying about recovering from a flood and a tornado. Maybe they've forgotten about it," said Fred.

42

Wedding

Six Weeks Later

Fred and Oscar were once more having coffee at the Country Cooking Restaurant in Willow River.

"This is getting a bit boring," said Fred as the two old-timers sat down at their reserved table for their weekly breakfast meeting. They discovered that the Country Cooking Restaurant in Willow River lacked the rich ambiance they had enjoyed for several years at the Black Oak Café in Link Lake.

"What's gettin' boring?" asked Oscar.

"First, it's a long drive over here. It's at least eight miles. Burning up a lot of gas just to have some breakfast."

"Well, Fred. We could ride together and take turns driving over here," said Oscar.

"What fun would that be?" said Fred, with a smile that split his wrinkled face from one side to the other.

"So have you heard the news? Lots of news swirling around these days," said Oscar.

"So you gonna tell me about it, or do I have to just sit here sipping coffee and wondering what is happening in the world?" said Fred.

Oscar took a big sip of coffee, set down his cup, and wiped his face with his napkin. "First off, did you hear that they are about finished building a spanking new restaurant in downtown Link Lake?" said Oscar.

"Really? I'd heard that folks owning the place were giving up on Link Lake and buying a restaurant in Waupaca," said Fred.

"Nope, you heard wrong. They have changed the name just a little. It will now be known as the Old Oak Café," said Oscar. "Right in the same spot they were before the tornado flattened them."

"Hope they got to save the recipes that made the old place popular," said Fred.

"I'm sure they have," said Oscar. "And I've got more news, too."

"More news, huh? You are one newsy guy this morning," Fred said, chewing on a piece of overdone toast. "Let's hear it."

"Jackie Jo from the library and the school teacher are getting married," said Oscar.

"Well, about time," Fred said.

"Why do you say that?"

"Most people in town know that our cute little librarian has been shacking up at the Williams House with that high school teacher for several months now, living together like they were married when we all knew they weren't."

"Fred, Fred," said Oscar as he put his hand on his old friend's arm. "You are sounding like the 1930s. This is the 2000s. Young people do things differently these days. At least these two are getting married. Some young couples just live together and never marry."

Fred just shook his head and continued eating. After a few minutes, he said, "So when and where are they getting married?"

"The when is next Saturday, and the where is the Church of Peace, since the big old church was never touched by the flood or the tornado."

"Is that right?" said Fred. "I happen to know Pastor Ezra Brown. He was a member of the writers' group at the library before the tornado tore into town. An interesting guy, once you get to know him."

"So are you going to the wedding?" Oscar asked.

"Yup, I'll be there. And you should be there as well. Jackie Jo needs all the support we can give her—old Mayor Olaf, now gone, wasn't too keen on there even being a library in Link Lake."

✐

The day of the wedding dawned sunny and clear. The wedding was scheduled to start at eleven, with a meal following at noon and a big wedding dance at the cultural arts center scheduled for the evening.

In the months following the flood and tornado, Jackie Jo had been working with Susan Frederick, director of the cultural arts center. They were looking beyond the cleanup and rebuilding of downtown Link Lake for events that involved both the library and the arts center. Jackie Jo asked Susan to be her matron of honor for the wedding. Ben asked Susan's husband, Deputy Sheriff Matt Higgens, to be his best man. Ben and Jackie Jo had become good friends with Susan and Matt. Beyond the various work projects the women were working on together, the two couples often went out for fish together on Friday evenings.

The day before the wedding, Jackie Jo's parents arrived in Link Lake from Columbus, Ohio, where Jackie Jo had grown up. They were surprised at how small Link Lake was and how friendly the people were. They had known about the flood and tornado and were quite surprised by how everyone was adjusting to all the changes that were taking place in the town. Ben's parents also arrived from Chicago for the wedding. Jackie Jo had arranged for both couples to have rooms at the Lake View Motel in Willow River.

When Fred and Oscar arrived at the church on the hill, as they called it, the pews were already nearly filled. With all of the troubles the village had experienced during the last several months, from a flood to a recalled election for mayor to a tornado that ripped apart the downtown, people in Link Lake continued to like celebrations, especially weddings.

Fred and Oscar found seats near the back of the church, and they were only seated a few minutes when the organist began playing "Here Comes the Bride." Jackie Jo, in a beautiful white dress and on the arm of her tall, thin father dressed in a black tuxedo, began walking down the aisle with all eyes in the church turned toward them. Ben's best man, Matt Higgins, and Jackie Jo's matron of honor, Susan Frederick, along with Pastor Brown, stood waiting in front of the altar.

When everyone was in place, and Jackie Jo's father was seated with her mother in one of the front rows, Pastor Brown began speaking in a loud, clear voice, "Thank you all for coming on this beautiful day. I can't remember when the church was this filled with people."

The pastor's voice was interrupted by a little boy running down the aisle and yelling, "Mommy, Mommy." It was Susan and Matt's little boy, Josh, who had escaped from the couple who had agreed to look after him during the wedding ceremony.

When he reached his mother, she bent down, gathered him up, and kissed him on the cheek. The wedding ceremony began with Pastor Brown's words: "We are gathered here today to join together Jackie Jo Jensen and Benjamin Neverson in holy matrimony." And ending with the words, "Do you, Jackie Jo Jensen, take Benjamin Neverson to be your lawfully wedded husband and cherish him in sickness and in health, until death do you part?"

"Yes," said Jackie Jo, holding back tears.

Pastor Brown then looked at Ben. "Do you, Benjamin Neverson, take Jackie Jo Jensen to be your lawfully wedded wife and cherish her in sickness and in health, until death do you part?"

"Yes," answered Ben, with a big smile spreading across his face.

After the exchange of rings, Pastor Brown announced Jackie Jo and Ben husband and wife and said, "You may now kiss!" which they did. The newly married couple started walking down the aisle with the best man and matron of honor following behind. Little Josh, holding his mommy's hand, skipped alongside her on their way to the church door.

Everyone walked a few blocks to the newly remodeled and re-roofed Increase Joseph Memorial Library, where lunch was served in the enlarged community room. Though not yet open for business, the newly constructed Old Oak Café catered the food—the first event for the newly constructed Main Street restaurant.

43

A Village Looking Ahead

"So whaddya think, Fred?" Oscar asked as the two old farmers found an empty table in the back of the newly opened Old Oak Café.

"About what? My mind's been filled with thoughts these days. Lots goin' on in old Link Lake. Some of the place is brand new, like this restaurant."

"Let's start with this place. Any comments about it? I know you were not too happy with the restaurant in Willow River."

"I was gettin' fed up with that place—pardon the pun," said Fred.

Oscar smiled. "So how do you like this new place?"

"It's okay, but it will take some gettin' used to. I'm not too comfortable around new things. They usually mean I've gotta make some adjustments in my life," said Fred.

"Okay, Fred. What's one thing you really like about this place?" asked Oscar.

"It's close. Don't have to waste gas money driving here."

They both sat quietly eating when Pauline stopped by with coffee refills.

"Good to see you guys," said Pauline. "It's been a while."

"Glad to be here," said Oscar. "Link Lake folks are a tough bunch. They're not gonna let a flood and a twister spoil their future."

"You've got that right," said Pauline as she finished filling coffee cups and moved on.

"So what'd you think about the big wedding?" asked Oscar.

"It was okay. Big crowd. Church was full. So was the community room at the library. You know what I liked best about the wedding, Oscar? The very best part?"

"I can't imagine," Oscar said as he chased a bit of bacon around his plate.

"That little boy yelling 'Mommy' and running up to her in the wedding party. He is sure a cute little bugger. I don't think anybody minded much that he did that either," said Fred.

"You been in the library since they remodeled, enlarged, and put on a new roof?" asked Oscar.

"Nope. Wedding reception was the first time. It's really changed. Lots bigger than what it was. Jackie Jo's money-raising program must have worked well. It took a bunch of bucks to do what's been done to the library. Let's see, a new reading room. A much larger community room, a room for kids with a bunch of kids' books, and a special computer room.

"To change the subject," Fred continued. "What's your take on the interim mayor, Karl Lightman, who took over when old Olaf Knudson kicked the bucket? He was head of the town council, as you know."

"I don't know him very well. He's one of those younger guys elected when Jon Jessup won the mayor's race. One of the things he did, and I applaud him for doing it, is bring the former Planning Commission back. We met for the first time since Olaf pulled the plug on the commission and what we were doing. When Jon Jessup was mayor, he chaired the commission. And you know what?" Oscar asked.

"I'll bet you're gonna tell me."

"Jon Jessup is chairing the Planning Commission again. Our interim mayor asked him if he would do it, and he said yes."

"Really? I thought he would be so ticked off from losing the recall election that he didn't want anything to do with local government anymore," said Fred.

"Do you know what he said when we all sat down to meet the other day?"

"I imagine he ranted on about how he had lost the recall election," said Fred.

"Nope," said Oscar. "He looked around the room, and everybody was there except Ben Neverson, who was off on a couple of weeks' honeymoon. Jon said, while rolling up his sleeves, 'Now, where were we? We've got lots of work to do.' That's what he said. Everybody on the Planning Commission clapped."

Epilogue

A Month Later

Ethyl Williams, longtime volunteer at the Increase Joseph Memorial Library, sat at the checkout desk. It was shortly after the library opened on this Monday morning. The library was empty except for a couple of people working on computers in the new computer room. Ethyl was thinking back to all that had happened in the previous months, from the flood that ruined several homes in Link Lake to the recent tornado that ripped the roof off the library and left the cultural arts center with little damage but destroyed all the other businesses on Main Street, including the Black Oak Café and the Link Lake Tap, popular gathering places.

Ethyl looked around the shiny new-looking library and smiled. She had a secret that only she and her twin sister knew for many years until the flood left several feet of dirty water in the library basement, and Jackie Jo discovered the stolen bank money in a waterproof bag floating in the basement floodwater. She remembers the stories she heard about the bank robbery in 1940 and the mystery of what happened to the robber's money. No one knew that the handsome young man posing as someone looking for work was a bank robber and that he and the Williams twins were the result of her mother taking a liking to the young robber. They were born nine months after he was caught and sent to prison in Waupun, where he died.

Ethyl remembered it as if it were yesterday. Her mother, Phoebe Williams, sat the twins down when they were sixteen and said she had something to tell them. They imagined she wanted to talk about them beginning to date and what they should do and what they definitely should not do. But that was not what their mother wanted to talk about.

Phoebe began once all three were seated in the Williams' living room.

"I have something to tell you that I want you to share with no one," she said. "I know you both have been wondering who your father was and where he is now. I know your classmates at Link Lake High have asked you that question often. I know you have come home from school asking questions about your father, which I always avoided answering.

Your father was the man who robbed the bank in 1940. You are to share that information with no one, absolutely no one."

Both Emily and Ethyl gasped when they heard the news. Never did they guess that their father was the 1940 bank robber who spent most of his life in the Waupun Prison and eventually died there.

"The second secret that you must never, ever share with anyone is this," Phoebe said, taking a deep breath and looking at her twin daughters for a reaction.

"Did you hear what I just said?" their mother asked.

In unison, the twin sisters said, "Yes, we heard."

"Before the police caught up with (his new name here), he left the money he stole with me."

"He what?" the sisters asked.

"He left the stolen money with me," their mother answered.

"How much money was it?" Emily asked.

"I don't know. I remember it being in a canvas bag with the words 'Link Lake Bank' on it. I never opened the bag."

"What did you do with the bag of money?" Ethyl asked.

"I was volunteering at the library then. I arrived at the library before it opened and stored it in a corner of the basement. That's one of the main reasons I always wanted one of you to volunteer at the library—so you could make sure the money was safe."

As Ethyl sat thinking on this particular morning, she had a moment where she thought, *That's what happened.* Jackie Jo must have found the sack of money, which the floodwaters dislodged from its hiding place, and she was using the money to make improvements to the library. She couldn't imagine that the gifts and grants coming to the library after the tornado would come close to the amount of money spent on the library improvements. Jackie Jo was putting the robbery money to good use.

Ethyl smiled. She wouldn't tell Jackie Jo that she knew all about the robbery money and now believed Jackie Jo was one more person who knew the answer to the Link Lake mystery: Who has the money left behind by the 1940 bank robber?

Acknowledgments

Writing a novel requires the help of many. First, I want to thank my late wife Ruth, who passed away during the time that I was working on this book. She, herself an extension agent at one time, offered many suggestions on what to include. We first met when I was an extension agent in Green Lake County, and she was an extension agent in Waushara County, a neighboring county to the north. My daughter Susan, an author of several books, and an excellent editor, helped me more than she will ever know as I continued writing after Ruth's passing. Natasha Kussulke, my daughter-in-law, a trained journalist, provided many useful tips including the title for the book. Steve, her husband and my son offered many big picture ideas for the story. From his office in Colorado, my other son, Jeff, patiently listened when I shared several of my concerns about the book with him. And lastly, I can't say enough of how I appreciate the hard work of Kristin Mitchell and her staff at Little Creek Press for agreeing to publish this work, and provide several ideas for making my rough draft manuscript better. Thank you.

About the Author

Jerry Apps was born and raised on a farm in central Wisconsin. Upon graduation from the University of Wisconsin-Madison, and spending time in the U.S. Army, Apps worked as a county extension agent in Green Lake and Brown County Wisconsin. He then worked as a staff development specialist for the University of Wisconsin-Extension. He is Professor Emeritus of the University Wisconsin-Madison and the author of several fiction and non-fiction books about agriculture and rural life in the Upper Midwest.

Printed in the United States
by Baker & Taylor Publisher Services